"I'll call this dog shrink."

Selena sighed. "But if he shows the first sign of training the joy out of Axel, he's gone. I may not want my sofa in shreds, but if I'd wanted a robot, I would have bought one of those electronic pets."

Robert came back with a name and phone number on a slip of paper. He gave the paper to Selena and a rather soulful kiss to Margo before returning to the counter.

Margo's expression turned dreamy. "What a lovely man."

"The dog shrink?"

"No, silly. Robert. And he has really nice friends. Just say the word—"

"No, thank you! Not everyone is cut out to be part of a couple. Two males in my life are enough, even if one's a dog."

Margo laughed. "Selena, my friend, someday love is going to sneak up and catch you so unaware. I, for one, would pay to see that show."

"How about you pay to see a more likely show? When Axel makes short work of this—" Selena glanced at the slip of paper "—Jack Quinn."

Dear Reader,

Blame It on the Dog was the most fun I've ever had writing! Not only did I get to brainstorm with four extremely talented writers as we created the SINGLES…WITH KIDS series, but I got to "go to work" every day in San Francisco, a city where anything is possible.

As creative and free-spirited as Selena is, I knew she'd need a hero who would not be deterred either by her staunch independence or her emotional intensity. I've always been drawn to the strong, silent type, so Jack was never far from my subconscious. He has his work cut out for him, what with Selena, her adolescent son, Drew, and their overly exuberant mutt Axel, and, even as I wrote the last sentence, I was never thoroughly certain who tamed whom. I hope you enjoy reading this story as much as I enjoyed writing it!

All my best,

Amy

P.S. As a result of writing *Blame It on the Dog*, I adopted a dog from our community shelter. When Ozzie first arrived in our home, he was every bit as lovable as Axel—and every bit as undisciplined! As my husband and I walked him to establish pack leadership, we rekindled our own relationship. So romance begets romance!

BLAME IT ON THE DOG
Amy Frazier

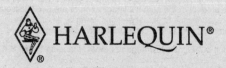

TORONTO • NEW YORK • LONDON
AMSTERDAM • PARIS • SYDNEY • HAMBURG
STOCKHOLM • ATHENS • TOKYO • MILAN • MADRID
PRAGUE • WARSAW • BUDAPEST • AUCKLAND

ISBN-13: 978-0-373-78168-3
ISBN-10: 0-373-78168-7

BLAME IT ON THE DOG

ABOUT THE AUTHOR

Having worked at various times as a teacher, a media specialist, a professional storyteller and a freelance artist, Amy Frazier now writes full-time. She lives in Georgia with her husband, two philosophical cats and one very rascally terrier-mix dog.

Books by Amy Frazier

HARLEQUIN SUPERROMANCE

Don't miss any of our special offers. Write to us at the following address for information on our newest releases.

Harlequin Reader Service
U.S.: 3010 Walden Ave., P.O. Box 1325, Buffalo, NY 14269
Canadian: P.O. Box 609, Fort Erie, Ont. L2A 5X3

An appreciative fan deserves a little fanfare.
Betty Ann D., this book is for you!
I hope it meets your expectations.

CHAPTER ONE

THE CRASH RATTLED the light fixtures in Selena Milano's loft apartment and made the CD player skip. Earthquake? Twelve-year-old son? Or dog? Betting dog, she turned from the end of the apartment that served as her studio and took a step toward the ruckus. It wouldn't be the first time she had to recycle the remnants of an Axel accident into one of her pieces.

"Drew! Are you okay?"

The response from the area of the loft partitioned to create her son's sleeping quarters wasn't good. Barking. Laughter. And a scraping noise that sounded as if someone was dragging a barge across the hardwood floor.

"Drew!"

"Chill, Mom, we're okay."

She didn't believe that for a minute.

Fortunately, their oversized apartment in a rehabbed city block in the Mission District had once housed a small garment factory. Delicate it wasn't, which was good because her family of three seemed to require industrial strength.

"I'm almost finished here!" she shouted above the persistent noise. "Why don't you get Axel on his leash? Take him downstairs and wait on the sidewalk, but don't get near Sam's produce." Sam was the greengrocer in one of the storefronts under the apartment, and Axel's nonstop tail always came perilously close to destroying the perfect pyramids of fruit and vegetables Sam erected on his outdoor display counters every morning. Although the *Chronicle* had reported nearly one half of San Francisco voters were dog owners, Selena seemed to have drawn the one block that had little tolerance for the critters.

Axel himself, one hundred pounds of sheer canine energy, burst out of Drew's sleeping area and charged the length of the apartment, his leash whipping behind him, clearing the landscape like a bulldozer carving a new suburban subdivision. Several feet away from her, he reared up to plant his front paws on her shoulder. Turning her head to avoid his kiss, she smelled the grape jelly before she saw it on his hairy right foot.

Drew appeared seconds later. "Are you ready?"

Longing for the quiet retreat that was Margo's Bistro, Selena pushed Axel toward Drew. "Wash his feet in the work sink. I'll meet you outside after I've tried to rescue this top." Examining the purple smear on her shoulder, she headed for the lavatory. "And don't let go of the leash."

That dog. Rescuing him had seemed like such a good idea when Margo had found him half-starved and rummaging in the garbage behind her café. Kindhearted Margo would have taken him in, but she had enough on her plate at the time. So she'd offered him to Selena, who'd been having trouble with Drew and his emerging adolescent angst. Margo thought caring for a pet would help draw him out of his self-involvement. Boy and dog had bonded beautifully. One could call it a growing relationship. The vet had laughed at Selena when she'd brought what she'd thought was a small, but fully grown dog for the necessary shots. Seems Axel was a very large, but emaciated, puppy at the time. Now, ten months and several tons of dog food later, he was a gigantic specimen of overgrown-pup exuberance.

Drew wanted her to do a portrait of his beloved pet. But what materials would convey his size and extraordinary coat? Two-by-fours, an old beer keg and a bale of pine needles?

Unable to eliminate the jelly stain, Selena changed into a clean but worn sweatshirt— why did she never seem to be able to keep clothes new and pretty?—threw on a jacket, grabbed an umbrella, then dashed outside to meet her son. Drew kicked a Hacky Sack on the crowded sidewalk as Axel, tied by his leash to a bike rack, cavorted about, barking loudly and threatening to overturn the rack and a half-dozen bikes. Sam stood outside his shop and eyed both boy and dog uneasily.

"Come on." Untying Axel, Selena urged her son away from the store.

The dog lunged ahead, dragging Selena and narrowly missing a couple heading into the tattoo parlor. Constantly chasing after this mutt, why wasn't she a size two?

Although the rain hadn't started yet, February clouds loomed ominously. It would be quicker to take BART, the underground transit system, but it only allowed service dogs. Her arm pulled nearly out of its socket, Selena harrumphed at the thought of Axel serving anyone but his own dogged interests, which consisted of eating, sleeping and running and jumping, followed by more running and jumping. Drew wanted to take him to the annual Blessing of the Animals on the Feast of St. Francis, but Axel was so ill-behaved Selena despaired of ever making that date. Sadly, their pet would try the patience of even a dead and sainted animal advocate.

Blocks later, the only reason Axel stopped in front of Margo's Bistro was that he knew Margo or Robert or one of their kids would have a biscuit for him if he stood still and looked pathetic.

"Do you want me to get you something?" Selena asked, handing Drew the leash. After one afternoon of busing tables—before the customers had had a chance to eat the food themselves—Axel was doggie-non-grata inside Margo's during business hours.

"A ginger-peach smoothie. And, Mom, do you know you have toilet paper stuck to your shoe?"

She looked down at her feet to see a long, white streamer trailing from one heel. Not surprised, but exasperated nonetheless, she bent to remove the offending accessory, then tossed it in the trash can. "Hold on to Axel. I'm going in."

Too late. The café door opened, and a customer came out. The scrabble of claws on the pavement warned Selena that Drew didn't have control of his dog. When did he ever? Before she could sound the alarm, the overgrown mutt knocked the man aside, then burst through the doorway, shedding hair and shaking drool and looking for the biscuit that was his due.

A teenager at the counter screamed. Robert stepped protectively in front of the girl as Margo reached for a broom. Axel took the move as an invitation to play and, grabbing the bristles, proceeded to drag Margo for a turn around the café. Selena tried to grab Axel's collar, but the dog, delighted that everyone found this game as much fun as he did, spun around and planted his front paws on Selena's shoulders for the second time that day.

"Hey, you two," Robert called out, trying not to laugh. "We're only a café. We don't have a permit for dancing."

Her son managed to pull his dog to a sitting position.

Margo shook her broom at Drew. "Your mother doesn't give you an allowance big enough to buy this monster a leash?"

Drew held up the broken end of the now useless restraint. "The third one this week."

"Oh, no," Selena moaned. "Now how are you going to take him to the park?"

"I'll use my belt."

He might as well. The thing never seemed to hold up his pants.

"And you—" Margo shook her broom at Axel, who now lolled belly-up on the floor at Drew's feet "—I'm not sure you deserve a cookie."

"Aw," Robert said, "can't you see he's

wasting away to nothing? Skin and bones." He reached behind the counter, then palmed a biscuit to Drew. "Give it to him in the park. After he's done something he's supposed to, for a change. So what'll you have, kid?"

"I was going to have a smoothie," Drew replied, eyeing another customer walking through the door, "but I think I'll just grab a Snapple and head out. Mom's paying." Bottle in hand, he shrugged away from Selena's attempted kiss.

"I have a meeting with a sponsor at noon," she said after his retreating form. "Pick me up in an hour, but wait outside this time." She resisted the urge to tell him to zip up his jacket. To ask if he'd remembered gloves. If he wanted the umbrella. Twelve-year-olds were a universe apart from eleven-year-olds in what they would tolerate from Mom. Pity. At times she missed her little boy.

As the door shut behind the pair, warmth and peace descended on the café. Selena desperately needed some quiet time with adults. Ever since she'd walked into Margo's Bistro from an installation she was doing in SOMA, the café had become a touchstone. A safe haven. A place where no one was a stranger for long.

Robert stepped behind the counter, and as Margo put away her broom, she surreptitiously ran her hand down his back. Selena smiled. Robert, a former flat-out workaholic, had wandered into Margo's Bistro ten months ago to read the want ads over a cup of coffee. He hadn't counted on falling for Margo and being swept up in her definitely noncorporate way of life. But did he ever look happy now. Not even a visit from Axel the Demolition Dog could eradicate the smile marriage to Margo had put on his face.

Selena flopped into one of the two overstuffed armchairs by the front window. When Margo joined her in the chair opposite, Selena asked, "Is it too early for Irish coffee?"

"A wee bit. And every time you ask you seem to conveniently forget we don't have a liquor license."

"You can't blame a girl for suggesting."

"Rough week?"

"No more than usual. You know that controlled chaos I call my life? I think I'm losing the controlled part." Glancing around the crowded room, Selena didn't see any of the friends who made up their core circle. "Where is everybody?"

"Well," Margo replied, stretching slowly and luxuriously as if she were the most contented woman in the world, "Rosie and Hud are still on honeymoon. A working honeymoon, some political retreat in D.C. Casey's staying with Bailey and Derrick, who've taken all the kids to Fisherman's Wharf today. Say a little prayer for those brave souls. And Nora and Erik are at a medical conference in Lake Tahoe. Nora's sister has Danny."

Pairs. Selena was struck by the realization the once tight single-parents coffee group had become a loose confederation of married friends who got together when new, blended and extended family commitments allowed.

And she was the last staunchly single person standing.

"And Ellie and Peter?" she asked before she could examine how she felt about being left behind. "Is it your ex's weekend to have them?"

"Yes. Tom and Catherine are taking the kids to look at prospective summer camps."

Selena was pleased to see Margo finally speak of her custody arrangement without a trace of stress.

"So you have my undivided attention," Margo promised, "and Robert's on call if we need him."

As if on cue, Robert brought two cups of coffee, a double mocha with vanilla whipped cream for Margo and espresso for Selena. "Your usual, ladies. Apart from the dog-and-pony show, Selena, how's it going?"

"Fine. Only if you don't count the dog."

"Oh, that sweet baby," Margo cooed in exaggerated admiration. "You can't stay mad at him."

"You don't live with him. And my neighbors aren't as forgiving as you two." Selena sipped her high-octane drink. "I know I wasn't a dog-savvy person when I agreed to take him, but who knew he'd grow this big?"

"You didn't notice the size of his paws when we found him?"

"You did?"

"Well, it occurred to me…." Margo suppressed a grin.

"What's the latest?" Robert asked. "Besides the exhibition here this morning."

"This week he ate the cushions on my sofa." Selena shuddered to remember. "And the mail. Five days running. I was so worried about the possible effects—on him—I took him to the vet for X rays. Dr. Wong says Axel has a cast-iron intestinal tract, if you're interested. Then I received three calls from neighbors about his barking. And, last but not least, yesterday he ran off two students from the dance studio next to Sam's. I owe for their missed lesson."

"He may be bored," Margo suggested.

"How can he be bored when he has Drew for a constant companion? And the two of them never stop moving."

"Does Drew walk him every day?"

"Walk? Hah! They run everywhere. It's only a matter of time before they knock someone over, and I have a lawsuit on my hands."

Robert sat on the arm of Margo's chair. "Sounds like Axel needs an obedience class."

"Obedience. What a nasty word," Selena replied with a frown. "I don't want to break his spirit."

"But if he breaks his leash once too often, he's going to land in the pound," Margo protested. "And then how will Drew feel?"

"Awful. Simply awful. Me, too."

"You always say you love controlled chaos. Sounds like it's time you take control of your dog before a solution is imposed upon you. One you might not like."

Margo had touched a nerve. She knew just how much Selena hated being backed into a corner. Being told what to do and how to do it.

"I may have a solution," Robert said. "I have a friend with an older brother who's a dog trainer. Or psychologist, I'm not sure which. But he has an impressive list of clients. I could get his number for you."

"A dog shrink?" Selena was skeptical. "Sounds a little too California even for me. Is he on the level?"

"Absolutely. I've met him. He's as no-nonsense as they come. Besides his private consultations, he rescues and rehabilitates stray and feral dogs."

"He doesn't sound flaky," Margo insisted. "He sounds compassionate."

Robert rose to wait on a customer. "I'll get his number for you before you leave."

Selena remained unconvinced. "I really think Axel will grow out of it," she said to Margo. "Don't they say that from eight months to three years dogs are adolescents? So he's really Drew's age. The two of them are growing so fast they can't control their own bodies. And I don't expect Drew will be on an emotional roller coaster forever. He'll mature and settle down. So will Axel. Nature has a way of sorting these things out."

"If you say so."

"You're giving me that look."

"What look?"

"The one that says I'm being stubborn."

"You said it, I didn't."

Selena sighed. "I'll call this dog shrink. But if he shows the first sign of training the joy out of Axel, he's gone. I may not want my sofa in shreds, but if I'd wanted a robot, I would have bought one of those electronic pets."

Robert came back with a name and phone number on a slip of paper. He gave the paper to Selena and a rather soulful kiss to Margo before returning to the counter.

Margo's expression turned dreamy. "What a lovely man."

"The dog shrink?"

"No, silly. Robert. And he has really nice friends. Just say the word—"

"No, thank you! Not everyone is cut out to be part of a couple. Two males in my life are enough, even if one's a dog."

Margo laughed. "Selena, my friend, some day love is going to sneak up on you and catch you so unaware. I, for one, would pay to see that show."

"How about you pay to see a more likely show? When Axel makes short work of this—" Selena glanced at the slip of paper "—Jack Quinn."

HE WAS STRUCK not so much by the sullen adolescent who opened the door, but by the overwhelming clutter and confusion of the apartment behind the kid. Even that impression took a backseat to the powerful baying of an unseen dog miserable at being shut away somewhere. The distinct smell of acetylene hung in the air, giving the whole situation a decidedly film noir feel.

"I'm Jack Quinn," he said, extending his hand. "I'm here to talk about Axel."

The boy ignored the offered hand. "Mom! He's here!"

Jack looked toward the far end of the large loft where a figure turned, removed a welding helmet and put down a torch. A woman. As she approached, she unzipped a paint-spattered coverall. A riot of short dark curls framed a face made exotic by large brown eyes and full lips. As she walked, she shrugged out of the coverall, an act that looked for all the world like a butterfly emerging from her cocoon. He tried not to dwell on the sinuous movement of her arms and legs as she freed herself from the heavy outer garment. Underneath the drab coverall, she was dressed in a pink tank top and orange shorts, and although it was winter dreary and cold outside, a light sheen of perspiration covered her body, pulling her clothing to her curves. She kicked off red cowboy boots to reveal bare feet and hot pink painted toenails. Every movement was a kaleidoscope of sensuality.

He caught himself. How long had it been since he'd focused on a woman's looks? A long time.

"I'm Selena Milano." Seemingly unfazed by either the surrounding mess or noise, she stood before him in the doorway, her hand outstretched. "And this is my son, Drew. You can hear Axel. We put him in the bathroom until you tell us how this procedure works."

He took her hand and noted it wasn't delicate as he might expect from her appearance. It was substantial, her shake assertive, bringing him back to professional mode. The normal curiosity he always felt at the beginning of a case returned. Having worked with many troublesome dogs, he knew most of the problems arose not with the dogs but with the owners. His job with the dogs always proved easy. His role where the humans were concerned ended up as part detective, part diplomat, part counselor.

"Do you want to meet Axel now?" Selena asked, raising her voice to be heard over the dog's protests, but not indicating in any way Jack should enter the apartment.

"In a minute. First, I'd like to hear how you two see the problem."

To one side of the door, Drew remained a silent sentry, his eyes averted.

"I'm not sure it's a problem really," Selena said, unmoving. "He's just a big baby."

Baby or not, Jack bet the neighboring business owners and apartment dwellers considered the incessant howling a real issue. Especially now on a Tuesday evening, after a long day's work. "How old is he?"

"We're not exactly sure. He was a stray. The vet's best guess is about a year now, give or take a few weeks."

"Old enough to know better."

Selena bristled. "He had a very hard start to his life. He was a Dumpster dog. Because of that, we may have cut him some slack. But let me assure you, he's well loved now. A member of the family."

"He's a dog."

"Duh." Drew spoke for the first time.

"I'm not being sarcastic," Jack replied, beginning to feel uncomfortable standing just outside the loft. It was obvious these two had called him under pressure. There was nothing voluntary about this interview. He had to be careful how he handled their hostility if the dog was to get help. "Dogs are different than humans. They're pack animals and happiest when they have a strong leader. The best dog is a calm, submissive dog."

"Two of my least favorite words are dominance and submission," Selena snapped. "If these are your training techniques, I think you'd better leave."

"I'm not a dog trainer, I'm a dog behaviorist. If you give me a chance to explain the real nature of dogs and their needs, I think you'll see how we can address Axel's behavior. But if you want me to leave, I will."

She held his gaze for a long minute. "Since I've maxed out my credit card in advance for this visit, let's hear what you have to say. Come on in and sit down." She indicated a sofa, partially covered with a brightly colored throw and a huge pile of laundry.

When he sat, the corner of the throw flipped back, exposing a badly chewed cushion. Selena perched on a chair opposite as if the shambles of the room was a palace and she its queen. Drew slouched against the wall by the door, glowering at the adults. Axel's barking had deteriorated to a piteous moan.

"Is Axel neutered?" Jack asked.

"Of course," Selena replied as if this was an impertinent question from a rather dim courtier.

"Good." He needed to find some positive starting point. "You've already scored points as responsible pet owners."

From his lookout by the door, Drew rolled his eyes.

"What are the things Axel does that you'd like corrected?" he asked, persevering.

"Well…he chews everything," Selena answered, cautiously. "But maybe he's teething."

Jack noted the excuse as he glanced at the innumerable ratty chew toys strewn about the floor amid even more laundry and several half-eaten sneakers. "What else?"

"He jumps on people."

Drew moved a few steps away from the wall. "I don't mind when he jumps on me. He's only playing. He's not vicious or anything."

"Oh, no. Just the opposite," Selena added.

"He's awfully cute. You'll see. And affectionate. But he doesn't know his own strength, so you can't expect Mrs. Bierdermeyer, who's eighty-six and walks with a cane, to be as enthusiastic about his advances. We don't want to break Axel's spirit, but we don't want him to break Mrs. B's hip."

"Mrs. Bierdermeyer is a neighbor?"

"Yes."

"Do you only see her when you take Axel out?"

"Yes."

"So you're saying he's out of control even on a leash."

Selena tilted her chin imperiously upward. "We don't expect him to heel every minute if that's what you're getting at."

"Ah."

"What's that supposed to mean?"

"I think it's time I met Axel."

Selena narrowed her eyes. "Drew, please, let him out of the bathroom."

As the boy disappeared behind a partition, Jack stood to assume the calm, in-charge stance he used when meeting any new dog. "I'm going to observe. Pretend I'm not here."

"I don't think that will be poss—"

The apartment shook as a furry juggernaut burst into the room and caromed off the walls and furniture with Drew in hot pursuit.

"Axel, no!" Selena jumped up and joined the chase.

She'd described the dog as "cute." It wouldn't have been the description Jack would have used for the mixed breed. He loved dogs, but he didn't idealize them. This one in particular. The shaggy head of a terrier sat on the tan, barrel-chested body of a chow, punctuated by a chow's high, plumy tail. A herder's very long, strong legs completed the incongruous picture. Make that motion picture.

In a tangle of paws and feet, the boy wrestled the dog to the floor. It was obvious Axel loved every minute of the roughhousing. Finally, Selena snagged his collar. When Drew rolled out from under him and headed for the sofa, Axel followed, dragging Selena. The boy, the woman and the dog collapsed on the sofa with the dog stretched across both owners' laps, his tongue lolling from a mouth wide open in a silent canine laugh. It was clear who was in charge here. The queen had been dethroned.

"I can help you," Jack said simply.

Selena laughed, and the sound was music. "We don't care how he behaves inside! We just need a few training techniques so he can fly under the radar and not get in trouble when we take him out."

Looking at the absolute disarray in the apartment, so different from his own spare living quarters, he begged to differ. Animals and humans alike could benefit from order, routine, stability. Memory flickered. Of his own childhood with a military stepfather. As a boy he hated the constant moving, the impermanence. Ironically, what kept him from feeling lost and adrift in his movable world was the discipline his stepfather brought to the household. It was obvious how Axel handled the turmoil. Jack wondered how Drew handled it.

Selena cleared her throat.

"Ah…about Axel…" he said, unaccustomed to being caught off guard. "You have to exercise discipline before you exercise affection. I can teach you how."

"You mean we have to be cruel to be kind?" Selena's brief smile faded as she stroked Axel's floppy ear. "No, thanks."

"I'm not talking about cruelty. In any form." He wondered why the words discipline and submission had pushed this beautiful woman's buttons. "I'm talking about the natural order of things. In the animal world. Don't project human issues on your pet."

Too late he realized he'd been focusing on Selena to the exclusion of Drew, and that Drew had noticed.

Glaring at Jack, the boy pushed Axel off his lap and moved closer to Selena. Like a feisty little junkyard mutt protecting his territory. "I don't know, Mom," he said. "Maybe we don't need a dog shrink."

Jack ignored the insulting tone of voice. There was no mention or evidence of a Mr. Milano. By this kid's behavior alone, Jack would bet Drew had been the man of the house for some time. The dog needed help, sure, but not enough for Jack to step into the middle of possibly touchy family dynamics. The stepson of a man who'd never let go of the *step* distinction, Jack knew what it was like to guard from intruders the little bit you thought you owned.

He pulled a business card out of his pocket and handed it deliberately to Drew. "It's your dog, your decision," he said before moving toward the door. He could see Axel in the kitchen, rummaging through an overturned trash bin. "Call me if you change your mind. The fee that went on your charge card was for my standard three sessions. After today's consultation, if you decide to go elsewhere, I'll refund the price of two."

As he descended the stairs from the apartment, he thought of the woman above. In the five years since his wife Anneka's death, he'd worked with many women in an effort to rehabilitate their usually spoiled dogs. In the past year he'd begun to date. In all that time he hadn't met one woman who aroused a personal curiosity, no one for whom he regretted saying a final farewell. Until today.

Warmed by, but distrusting, this instant attraction to Selena Milano, he pushed through the building door to cool, moist air, into the neighborhood changing from bustling daytime business to early evening social.

Normally a solitary man, he found the sounds of music, the smell of food, the shouts from neighbor to neighbor jarring. If Selena interested him, why not ask her out? He knew why. Her son. Although Jack might be drawn to the woman, he'd be a fool to pursue even the most casual relationship in the face of the boy's obvious antagonism.

CHAPTER TWO

WITH THE MOUTHWATERING aroma of tamales floating up from the *taquerías* across the street, Selena sat on a stool on the roof of her building, checking the fabric samples laid out in the open. They were for an upcoming installation on the campus of San Francisco State University. The theme was tolerance, and Selena envisioned scrims stretched taut on enormous frames planted in the earth. On one side would be a picture and personal statement by an ordinary person, describing a small, everyday act of tolerance. On the other a visual pulled from the headlines showing the stark reality of intolerance. She wanted the contrasting images imposed on opposing sides of fabric to highlight what little lay between the two directions. She didn't have the whole ideological thing worked out yet. Or even the execution. Right now she and Maxine, her assistant, were testing fabrics to find the one most likely to stand up to both the printing process and four weeks of San Francisco's ever-changing weather.

Drew had taken Axel for an after-school walk—well, run—in the park. For the past few days, he'd been committed to burning off some of his pal's energy. Neither Selena nor Drew wanted to have to bring back Jack Quinn and his boot-camp ideas. Trouble was the outings seemed to be stoking Axel's energy levels, not diminishing them.

With a groan, Maxine stood up. "I have to move around. You want some coffee?"

"Please. I made a fresh pot before we came up." Blowing on her hands, Selena watched Maxine head for the door to the stairway to the apartment below. Although it was probably fifty degrees, up here you caught the brisk winds off the Pacific. Coffee sounded good.

Maxine had been Selena's art teacher in high school. And when Selena had come back to San Francisco, pregnant, her old home sold, her parents off saving the world, Maxine had helped her find her first job at a community center, teaching adult education art classes. They'd stayed in touch, and when Maxine retired, she'd been eager to keep her artistic juices flowing as Selena's Jill-of-all-trades assistant. She was also the only grandparent figure Drew knew up close and personal.

"I put a little something in it," Maxine said, returning several minutes later with two mugs.

"Thanks." Selena would have to be careful. Maxine's "little somethings" could knock your socks off. And Selena was really only a two-glasses-of-wine imbiber.

Maxine leaned against the low brick wall that edged the roof. "So are you going to tell me about the dog shrink?"

Selena had been avoiding that subject. "I don't think he liked it when Drew called him that."

"The sensitive type. Well, pardon me."

"*Sensitive* is the last word I'd use to describe this guy. If I had to pick only one word, it would be controlling."

"Oh? Whips and masks?"

"He was more subtle. But controlling all the same. Not to mention frosty, smug and a tad dogmatic. Pun intended. Talked a lot about discipline and submission."

Maxine chuckled. "I'm assuming he was talking about Axel. And a little discipline wouldn't hurt that four-legged brat."

"You know how I feel about relationships—even cross-species relationships. They should be built on equality and mutual respect."

"Then I bet you and this guy got on like a house afire."

Selena grimaced at the unpleasant thought of Mr. I-Will-Teach-You-To-Be-Pack-Leader Quinn.

"Hey, Selena, give him a break. He's a dog trainer, for pity's sake. Someone's got to be in charge of the training. It might as well be the human."

"He didn't like being called a dog trainer, either."

"So what does he think he is?"

"I don't know. Some kind of Zen master, for all I know. It doesn't matter anyway. We gave him the boot."

"And your backup plan would be?"

"I don't have—"

Just then a crash and an ear-splitting shriek came from the sidewalk below, followed closely by a string of baritone expletives. Selena jumped up to peer over the wall and saw a river of fruit rolling in a cascade of oranges, yellows, greens and reds over the pavement and into the street.

Axel. She'd bet the farm.

She tore downstairs with Maxine on her heels. Outside, one of the stands that bracketed the produce market door lay overturned on the sidewalk. As Drew and several customers scrambled to right the stand and pick up the fruit, Sam raced around, waving his arms and chasing Axel, who held a grapefruit in his mouth and didn't seem to understand why Sam didn't want to play fetch.

On one of his run-bys, Selena grabbed Axel's collar, then Drew's sleeve. "Take him upstairs. Now. I'll settle with Sam." For once, Drew disappeared with his dog, without argument.

"Sam! Calm down!" Selena stepped in front of the red-faced man who seemed intent on following Axel right up into the apartment. "I'll clean this up. You tend to your customers."

"And what will they buy?" Sam growled. "My fruit is ruined!"

"Not all of it, I'm sure," Maxine said, stepping up to take Sam's arm, urging him into his shop. "Selena and I'll check every piece. If it's good we'll restack it."

"And if it's damaged, I'll pay for it," Selena added, her heart sinking. Bruised fruit could not be counted as a project expense. Now breakfast and lunch for the next week looked like smoothies, smoothies and more smoothies. "I'm sorry, Sam. I promise it won't happen again."

Maxine almost had the greengrocer inside his shop when he whirled to face Selena. "That dog of yours is a menace. A menace! Do you see Charlie?" Sam waved his arm in the direction of the homeless man across the street, pushing a grocery cart and leading a very large dog as homeless as he. Charlie and Pip existed on the kindness of those who lived and worked in the neighborhood. "Charlie's taught Pip more manners than most of the parents on this street have taught their kids. Why can't you control your dog, as well?"

Selena didn't have an answer to that.

A minivan with the city logo on the side pulled up, and a uniformed woman hopped out, a pole with capture-loop in hand.

"Oh, Sam!" Selena cried. "You didn't call Animal Control!"

"What else could he do?" Isadore, the owner of the dance studio, asked as a small crowd of neighbors began to gather. "Your dog's been a problem for all of us."

His remark was met with nods all around.

"Where's the dog?" the officer asked.

"My son took him upstairs," Selena replied. "Everything's under control."

"Everything's not under control," Sam snapped, indicating the fruit on the ground. "As you can see."

"Was the dog off-leash when this happened?" the officer asked.

"No," Sam admitted. "But a leash does no good. Her kid can't handle that overgrown mutt."

"Is this true, ma'am?"

"Occasionally…yes." What else could she say as her neighbors stared her down?

"Did he bite anyone?"

"No! He's not a biter!" Selena felt insulted on Axel's behalf.

"He's a barker!" Isadore exclaimed, warming to the exchange. "Day and night, night and day. Try teaching a dance class when you can hear his yapping over the music."

"And he never met a garbage can he couldn't overturn," someone at the back of the group groused. "Or a lamppost he didn't christen."

Selena felt outnumbered. "In our defense, we had a meeting with a dog behaviorist." She couldn't believe she was using the odious Jack Quinn to bolster her case. "He says he can turn the situation around. We signed up for three sessions." Semi-truth if you considered that, until now, she hadn't planned on seeing him again.

The control officer looked dubious. "Do you have a receipt?"

"Somewhere." Maybe.

"You'll need to bring it down to our offices. And, later, proof of course completion. Successful completion. There's a fine if you don't comply. Worst-case scenario if there are more complaints, we can impound the dog. So this is serious business. Understand?"

"I understand," Selena said with sinking heart.

The officer leaned the capture pole against the building, then pulled out a notebook. "In the meantime, I'm writing you a ticket. For disturbing the peace."

Selena knew this was the time to keep her mouth shut, but when she looked at the ticket, she couldn't contain herself. "A hundred bucks!"

"And you need to clean up this man's produce."

"I'll take care of it." Although, as she picked up and inspected Chilean and New Zealand kiwis, pomegranates and mangoes, she wasn't sure how. Other than asking Jack Quinn for help. More difficult than turning tail and admitting she might need that overbearing man was the thought of convincing Drew of the need.

Drew had liked Jack less than Selena had.

After restacking the saleable fruit and paying for two very large sacks of bruised items—Axel gave new meaning to the phrase "doggie bag"—Selena trudged up to her apartment.

"I'll finish up on the roof," Maxine said on the landing. "Call if you need reinforcements."

Inside the apartment an uncharacteristic silence met her. It seemed both boy and dog—who were nowhere to be seen—knew they'd stepped in deep doo-doo this time for sure. "Drew!"

"In here." She followed her son's dejected voice into his room.

He was sprawled on his bed next to Axel. A telephone book lay on the floor, open to the yellow pages. "I tried to find someone else, but there's no listing for dog shrink."

"No matter what Mr. Quinn calls himself, I think we'd have to look under dog training." Selena sat on the edge of the bed. "But we need to talk first."

"You don't really want to use this guy, do you?"

No, she didn't, but her reasons went beyond Jack Quinn's untested approach to Axel's reformation. "Why don't you want to use him?"

"I didn't like the way he looked at you."

So her son's reasons weren't too far from her own. Except she didn't know how she felt about the intense way Quinn looked at her. "He knows I'm the one paying," she offered in explanation. "I think he was trying to convince the comptroller Axel needs help." She rubbed the dog's belly. "But we already know that, don't we?"

"I guess. That doesn't mean we can't get help somewhere else."

"I've been thinking about that." This wasn't easy for her to admit. "First, Robert recommended this guy. And when I called Dr. Wong for a vet reference, she said he'd be her first choice, too. I wouldn't know any of these other people in the phone book or their qualifications. Second, I paid Quinn up front. I know he said we could get a refund, but that might end up a hassle. Third, remember it took a week and a half to get him over here? We need help now. If we have to wait another week-and-a-half to get someone new, Sam's not going to be happy. I bet I could call this Quinn character right now and tell him it's an emergency, and he'd set up our second visit, pronto."

"You think?"

"I won't get off the phone till he does."

Drew buried his face in Axel's hairy hide. "I saw Animal Control from the window. Are they gonna take him?"

"Only if we don't do something quick. I hate to admit it, but we already have the wheels in motion with this guy Quinn."

"Okay." Drew didn't sound in the least convinced. "Call him."

"Do you still have his card?"

Drew rummaged in his wastebasket and pulled out two ripped halves.

Selena took the pieces, then went into the kitchen to make the call.

He picked up on the first ring. "Jack Quinn here." She could imagine his deep-set eyes. His stern look relayed over air and wire to skewer her right here in her home.

"H-hello," she croaked. "This is Selena Milano. You were here a few days ago."

"I remember. Axel, right?"

"Right. Well…it seems we can use your help after all."

The long pause caught her off guard. "Mr. Quinn?"

"It's Jack. I was looking through my schedule. Do you want to come to my center for the second session next Tuesday?"

"Um…we sort of need something yesterday."

"Someone's lodged a complaint."

She hated that he was right. "Y-yes."

"I'm sensing, even with the complaint, you're not committed to this process."

"Oh, I am! It would break Drew's heart—and Axel's—if anything should separate them."

"All right. I can show you and your son everything Axel needs to be happy and well-adjusted. But are you willing to see Axel as a dog, not a furry child? Are you willing to follow my directions?"

She thought about this.

"Selena?" The quiet way he said her name sent shivers down her spine.

"I'm thinking."

"Well, think about this, too. Can you bring yourself to use the words *submission* and *discipline* without thinking of them as negatives?"

How dare he challenge her? She nearly hung up the phone until she remembered the threat of Animal Control. For Drew and Axel—not for Mr. Take Charge on the other end of the line—she finally said, "Yes." A qualified yes.

"I'm assuming you want Drew to be present. Tomorrow's Saturday. Come to my center at eleven, and I'll fit you in." He gave her the address in an industrial part of town. "Leave Axel at home."

The man was impossible. "Do you understand the emergency involves Axel? My neighbor isn't threatening to send my son and me to the pound."

"I understand. But we're not going to get anywhere with Axel until you understand a few basics. I want you to observe my pack of well-adjusted dogs."

His pack of dogs? What was this guy? Urban jungle boy? "And that's going to help our problem?" she asked, unable to keep the sarcasm from her voice.

"Absolutely. Trust me."

Oh, no. She might have agreed to follow his doggie-shrink routine for two more paid-up sessions, but trust him? She'd learned the hard way to trust no one but herself.

SELENA HATED missing Saturday mornings at Margo's. That was when she was most likely to run into friends. It seemed ages since she'd caught up with all the others, but the issue with Axel wouldn't go away. Maybe, if things went well at the dog center, Drew and she could stop in at the café later for scones.

The address Quinn had given her appeared to be a vacant lot between two warehouses. A high, chain-link fence backed by green tarp fronted the property. Stretched on the fence to one side of a wide roll-gate was a professionally painted banner that read Canine Rescue and Rehabilitation with a Web site below. Selena stepped up to a call box hanging next to the gate and pressed the button.

A voice—definitely not Quinn's deep rumble—said, "May I help you?"

"Selena and Drew Milano. We have an eleven o'clock appointment with Jack Quinn. I know we're a bit early, but I couldn't be sure how easy this place would be to find."

The gate swung open even as the disembodied voice replied, "No problem."

Selena and Drew stepped into an enclosed

area beautifully designed like a Japanese garden. There was the sound of running water, but not a dog in sight. A young man stepped out of a small building to greet them. "Jack said if you got here early, I was to give you a tour. He's working with a pretty intense case right now, but he'll be free shortly. I'm Andy. One of the assistants."

"How many people work here?" Selena was under the impression Jack worked alone with his pack of feral dogs. Out of his jungle-boy cave. In a loincloth.

"Three full-timers, including Jack. Three more part-timers. And a half-dozen interns. When it comes to dog issues, we're the go-to people." Andy looked quite proud of the fact. "When you're dealing with animals, it's a twenty-four-seven, year-round operation. And when you see the size of our resident pack, you'll see why we need a large crew."

"So where are the dogs?" Drew asked.

"Through the next gate." Andy indicated the chain-link fence on the far side of the garden. This fence was covered with tarp as well, so that what was on the other side remained a mystery.

"This is an unusual entrance for a dog center," Selena said, looking around at the contained yet peaceful landscape.

"Jack designed it with a purpose," Andy explained. "He believes dog owners must exhibit calm leadership. Even visitors to the center. The garden helps you relax and focus before you enter the dog compound." He led them toward the far gate. "There's one more holding area—for humans—but you can observe the pack from there."

"You keep talking about a pack. How many dogs are there?"

Andy grinned as he slid the second gate open. "You'll see."

Selena heard Drew gasp as they stepped into another smaller fenced-in area overlooking a compound the size of a football field neatly subdivided. In the very large section beyond the one in which they stood, dozens of dogs milled quietly about. Some lounged in the shade of awnings hung from the fenced perimeter. Others splashed in water-filled kiddy pools. Still others chased a ball in what looked like a canine game of pickup soccer. Selena was struck by the placid atmosphere even though the dogs were left to their own devices.

"There's no barking," Drew said in a near whisper.

"No," Andy replied. "These are well-adjusted dogs. But they weren't always like this."

As a group of dogs came up to the fence, curious to check out the visitors, Selena noted there wasn't a hyper Axel amongst them. No whining, barking or jumping on the chain link. As well-behaved as they were, however, she saw they weren't even city-pound-quality. Some were missing a leg, others an eye. Many of them bore ancient scars. "These guys aren't ever going to be adopted, are they?" she asked.

"It's doubtful," Andy replied. "But they have a home for the rest of their lives. Here. Jack's seen to that. He's even worked out a deal with the homeless in the area. If, for any reason, they can't take care of their dogs, they can bring them here. No questions asked. Even if it's just temporarily until the person thinks they can take care of the dog again."

Selena wasn't sure she was ready for Quinn to turn out to be a nice guy.

"Jack's working at the far end in one of the isolation pens," Andy said. "I'll give you the tour as we make our way to him."

"Through there?" Selena squeaked, as Andy moved to open the gate to the free-roaming dog area. Suddenly wading through a mass of street dogs seemed a little daunting.

"Sure," Andy replied. "You do know how to meet dogs for the first time?"

"There's a right way?"

"Absolutely." Andy looked especially at Drew, who seemed mesmerized by the pack. "No eye contact. No talking. No touching. At least until they've sniffed you thoroughly. Keep your head high, your shoulders back. Act like you own the world."

"Mom's good at that," Drew quipped.

"You'll do fine," Andy replied with a smile. "When we step through the gate, walk slowly toward the end of the compound, keeping your eyes on the top of that flagpole. I'll tell you when you can stop and interact."

She remembered how she'd just scooped up Axel as a pup and brought him home. If dogs were really this complicated they should issue owners' manuals. The thought gave her pause, but as Andy opened the gate, she took Drew's hand—it was testament to the power of the pack that he let her—and stepped into Jack Quinn's world.

She hadn't anticipated how difficult it would be to walk and not acknowledge the dogs she felt sniffing about her. Her first instinct, once she realized how truly well-behaved they were, was to greet them, pet them, get to know their individual personalities. But, having closed the gate, Andy walked alongside her with a hand on her back propelling her gently, silently forward. It all felt so ritualized she couldn't help wonder if she'd gotten herself involved in some canine cult.

"Okay," Andy said quietly. "Stop and look around."

What a letdown. Most of the dogs had wandered off to resume their previous activities. "What just happened?" she asked. "Or didn't."

"I'm assuming you have a dog who greets you differently."

"And how!" Drew said.

"They've acknowledged you as calm, assertive leaders," Andy explained. "Now they're just hanging out."

"But we don't want a dog that ignores us," Selena protested.

"Of course not." Andy whistled, and several dogs, tails wagging, responded quickly—still not jumping. He petted each in turn and urged Drew and Selena to do the same. "But you need to learn when to give affection. Always when a dog is calm. Giving it when the dog is overly excited just reinforces the unacceptable behavior."

Selena didn't know if she was buying in to this behavioristic rigmarole, but Drew seemed enamored of the circling dogs.

Andy glanced at his watch. "Jack should be about finished. Let's wind up the tour." He led them to yet another gate.

For the first time Selena noticed beyond the fenced-in dog area an outer walkway that connected the earlier holding area for humans to an area in the back where several people were bathing animals, while others worked with owners and their leashed pets. There was plenty of room left over for what looked like an agility training course and a semipermanent trailer with an Office sign hung by the door.

"You mean to tell me," she said, "we didn't have to walk through that sea of dogs?"

"Jack's orders."

Was the guy trying to intimidate her?

"Why is he in there?" Drew asked, pointing to a row of large cages at the far end of the property, each housing a single dog. Jack was in one of the pens with what looked like a spitz mix that had been muzzled.

Andy led them to stand a distance from the cages, then stopped. He spoke in hushed tones. "He's working with an abandoned dog. Very aggressive. The original rescuing shelter recommended he be put down as dangerous. But Jack rarely gives up on a dog. He thinks this one can be rehabilitated into our pack. The dog's accepted Jack's presence. Now Jack needs to show him who's leader."

Drew took a step forward, but Andy put a hand on his shoulder to stop him. "We can watch from here. But you're going to have to be very still. Radiate calm energy. Dogs can definitely sense otherwise. And you have to understand the struggle going on inside the pen involves no physical hurt to the animal. Jack's trying to put him on the ground. The ultimate submissive position for a dog."

Quinn controlled the large dog with what looked like an insubstantial leash looped high on the dog's neck behind the ears. Without speaking, Quinn slowly lowered the shortened leash to the ground, forcing the dog to lower its head. If Quinn was trying to get the dog to put its entire body on the ground in submission, however, the spitz was having none of it. After a few seconds with its head lowered, it would growl and thrash and manage to get to its feet. Quietly, Quinn would begin the procedure over again. At one point, he seemed to see an opportunity to bring the dog farther down. With the spitz's head on the ground and its eyes momentarily averted, Quinn encircled its chest and attempted to roll the dog on its back, all in a slow and silent, yet forceful, way that reminded Selena of a martial arts exercise.

Despite herself, she was now transfixed by the battle of wills between man and dog, fascinated by Quinn's patient strength.

Not Drew.

An appalled look on his face, he suddenly hurtled toward the cage. "Stop it!" he shouted, running forward and banging on the chain link. "You're hurting him! Stop!"

Startled, Quinn released the dog, who charged the fence, teeth bared inside the muzzle. As Andy pulled Drew back, Selena noticed that in the struggle to regain his footing, the spitz had sliced Quinn's nostril with one of its nails. Blood flowed from the trainer's nose onto his shirt as he slipped out of the pen, a barely restrained fury etched on his features. The spitz set up an unholy howling that reverberated throughout the compound and set the rest of the dogs barking in response. Handlers and owners could be heard, snapping commands to regain control of their animals.

Without a word, Quinn led Selena and Drew to the nearby trailer office as Andy trotted off toward the dog pack area.

Inside Quinn grabbed a bunch of tissues,

pressed them to his nose, then turned to Drew. "What you did was extremely dangerous." Although he didn't raise his voice, his words came out clipped and careful.

Selena could see by the blood soaking the tissue that her son's interruption had proven dangerous enough. "Here, let me look at your nose," she said, stepping forward, her nurturing instincts aroused.

"I'll be fine," Quinn replied and brushed her aside to focus on Drew. "Do you hear the rest of the dogs in the compound?" The barking had yet to stop. "Distress, fear, aggression can run through a pack like wildfire. You set off the spitz. He set off the rest. Even in a stable pack if an alarm is sounded, if members are unsure, they often lash out instinctively. Hurt before getting hurt. The dogs could hurt each other. Or their handlers. One false move, and I could have hurt the spitz."

"You *were* hurting him!" Shaking, Drew was close to tears.

"No. It was a natural struggle for dominance. For that dog to live with my pack— for him to live—he can't be the pack leader.

Not in his aggressive state. There's no question he'd eventually kill another member of the pack. He needs to submit to me as leader. Then there's no jockeying with the dogs. Then he can co-exist with the others. That's how it works in the dog world."

"You're making that up!" Drew spit back, unrepentant. "You're nothing but a bully, but you're not the boss of me! And I'm not letting you near my dog!" Before Selena could react, her son ran from the trailer.

When she attempted to follow, Quinn grasped her wrist. "Andy will take care of him."

Through the window she could see the assistant already with Drew, leading him along the outer walkway to the waiting area at the front of the compound.

"Do you think I was bullying the dog?" he asked, genuine concern showing in his dark eyes, making his chiseled features appear, if not softer, then at least less granite like.

She shook off his hand that still encircled her wrist. "No, I don't think you were bullying him." Although at this particular moment, with her son so upset, it was a hard admission for her to make. "Andy explained it's a very difficult case…but that you wouldn't hurt him."

"I'll help you with Axel. From what I saw, he won't require the technique you just observed. But you have to deal with Drew's issues as well."

"My son's issues?"

"He didn't just react. He overreacted. And the use of the word *bully*…maybe he feels picked on at school or in the neighborhood. Is that the case?"

"No!" At least she didn't think so. Besides, it wasn't any of this guy's business.

"Learning to be a good pack leader to Axel might make Drew feel more self-assured."

"Now you're saying my son's not self-assured?"

"I know the age. I've been there myself. One foot in boyhood, one in adulthood. Not sure where you belong. Not sure whether you can live up to the macho expectations of your peers and pop culture. I'm saying something set your son off just now. It might be wise to find out what."

Selena felt her maternal hackles rising. "Look, buddy, you might think of yourself as

Dog Yoda—though I'm not convinced I even want to put my dog under your control—but keep your pet psychobabble away from us humans. Nobody tells me how to raise my kid." In a self-righteous huff, she stormed out of the trailer in search of her son.

Jack watched her go, not so much surprised at her outburst, but at his own reaction to it. He should be angry at the challenge to his expertise. Or, at the very least, turned off by her arrogant behavior. He wasn't.

The smart course of action would be to write the Milanos off. He rubbed the back of his neck in frustration as he realized the opportunity to follow that very sensible path had passed. In his tumbling thoughts only one thing was clear. Now that he'd met her, it was impossible to disregard, dismiss or forget a woman like Selena.

CHAPTER THREE

SUNDAY MORNING, Selena stood outside Drew's closed bedroom door about to make yet another attempt at talking with her son. Yesterday when they'd come home, he'd given her the silent treatment. All afternoon and evening. He'd even refused a visit to Margo's Bistro, and, with his adolescent hollow leg, he never passed up a chance to eat one of Margo's magnificent creations. This morning he hadn't come out of his room. And, although she'd told Quinn to butt out of her business, she couldn't stop thinking about his words, couldn't help worrying there might be some truth to them.

"Drew, may I come in?"

When silence met her request, she cracked the door in case her son wore headphones and hadn't heard her. He lay across his bed, drawing, a cereal box tipped precariously on the edge of the nightstand, headphones nowhere in sight. Axel, ignoring his dog bed on the floor, lay across Drew's pillows, four enormous paws in the air.

She took a step into the room. "I'd like to talk to you."

"About what?"

"Anything you want." Sitting on the corner of the bed, she noticed an Axel-like superdog, complete with cape, dominated her son's drawing. Action-hero Axel vanquished a legion of robots who all bore a remarkable resemblance to Jack Quinn.

"I don't want to talk about anything," Drew said.

"Not even yesterday?"

He shook his head.

"What about school? We've been so busy lately we haven't had a chance to catch up. Anything I should know?"

He gave her a scathing look, one that told her in no uncertain terms he saw right through her nosy ploy, but he refused to answer.

Okay. About now, she could use some

advice from her friends with kids on finess-
ing words out of a reluctant twelve-year-old.
Without that advice, she'd have to resort to
her usual, not always successful candor.
"When you walk Axel alone…does anyone
give you a hard time?"

"You think?" Over his shoulder Drew
glanced at his dog taking up most of the bed.

Even asleep, snoring peacefully, the beast
looked like…well, a beast. Knowing what he
was like in motion, Selena honestly doubted
anyone messed with Drew in Axel's company.
But something was bugging her kid.

Where did the child who shared everything with her go?

The doorbell rang, waking Axel. It was
probably Maxine. They were supposed to
work on logistics for the SFSU installation.
Maybe in a grandmotherly role, Maxine
could get something out of Drew. When
Selena got up, so did Axel, who knocked the
box of cereal on the floor, spilling its
contents amidst the other preteen disorder.

The doorbell rang again, sending the dog
into paroxysms of barking on his way to
the door.

"I'm coming, I'm coming!" She pushed Axel out of the way. "If you'd remembered your key, we wouldn't have to go through—"

She opened the door not to Maxine, but to Jack Quinn.

As Axel barked and reared up on his hind feet, Quinn took a half step forward. Chest high, broad shoulders back, with a lock of dark hair falling over one eye, he looked more than a little intimidating. Axel must have felt the same because, amazingly, he stopped barking, put all fours on the ground and turned to leave. Quinn didn't let him. Before either Selena or Axel knew what was happening, the man reached out and secured the dog's collar, placed a firm hand on his rump, then put him in a sitting position. When Axel attempted to stand, Quinn merely put out his hand and uttered a quick, quiet, but commanding, "Hut!" Axel stayed. Moreover, his look went from stunned to adoring.

"How did you do that?" Selena asked, rather stunned herself.

"I've been trying to tell you it's not rocket

science." He held out a DVD. "Maybe if Drew looked at this—"

"I'm willing to talk, but not in the apartment." She looked over her shoulder to see if Drew had come out of his room. In his present state of mind, who knew how he'd react to Quinn's unexpected visit? She took the DVD, put it on top of the tall bookshelf next to the door where Axel couldn't get it, then pushed Quinn out onto the landing. She followed, shutting the door behind her.

Axel, on the other side, snuffled at the crack under the door. Knowing it wouldn't be long before he started to howl, Selena grabbed Quinn's arm and propelled him down the stairs, no easy feat as he was a tall, solidly built man. On the way down, they met Maxine coming up.

"I'll be back in a minute," Selena said before she had to make introductions.

Even so, in passing, Maxine gave Quinn the once-over as she did with all Selena's dates, then flashed a thumbs-up.

As if.

How could Maxine see this man as anything but the thorn-in-her-side he'd become?

She pushed Quinn through the downstairs doorway onto the sidewalk. "What's going on?" he asked.

The chill morning fog had yet to lift, and she wore nothing but a long-sleeved tee. To keep warm, she'd either have to jump up and down in front of Quinn like a woman gone mad or walk. "Let's walk," she said.

"Let me buy you a cup of coffee."

"No!" She didn't want to sit down anywhere with this guy. It would appear too normal. Dare she say too much like a first date? She wanted to hang onto the idea that he was, at most, a necessary evil. "A short walk's all we'll need."

"If you say so." Without asking, he took off his jacket and draped it over her shoulders.

She didn't want him to be thoughtful. And she certainly didn't want him to smell good. As his jacket did. Of leather and sandalwood. She tried to shrink from the lining which still held the heat of his body.

"Is this a bad time?" he asked.

"Yes. No. I don't know." After Maxine's appraisal, Selena was now all too conscious of Quinn's looks. He was handsome in a brooding, tortured-hero sort of way. What the hell was going on? This guy had already reduced Axel to a tail-wagging zombie. Now he'd reduced her to a blithering idiot. She nearly ran into a busker setting up his boombox, laying down plywood and a tip jar, getting ready to dance for the Sunday morning brunch crowd.

Jack observed Selena trotting erratically beside him and wondered what had her so on edge. "I know I should have called," he said, "but I thought the DVD was important. It's a documentary on the psychology of dogs. It shows the natural order of things in canine packs. I thought if you watched it with your son—if he got the information in a nonthreatening way—maybe he'd be willing to see what I have to offer."

When she didn't speak, he added, "Axel isn't a difficult case. We could take care of most of his issues with one session in the park. You saw how he responded just now in your apartment."

"Ah, yes, about that…what planet did you say you were from?"

He felt a laugh begin in his chest. A

strange sensation. "You need to watch the DVD, then I'll answer all your questions at our next session."

"You seem certain there will be a next session."

He wasn't certain. He was making it up as he went. To prolong the walk. With her. "It depends on Drew. Kids his age are usually fascinated with animals. Use the DVD to draw him into the process."

"So now you're an expert on kids as well as dogs. Do you have any of your own? Kids, that is."

"No." He didn't want to get into the fact that he wasn't sure he should have kids. He hadn't had the best of father models. "Let's just say I think both Drew and you really want what's best for Axel…but neither of you wants to admit what you've been doing hasn't worked out the way you'd like."

"Are you always so sure of yourself?"

He could have asked her if she was always so defensive, but he didn't want to risk driving her away. "I know dogs. And I've worked with enough dog owners to understand their reservations."

"Their reservations until they discover the 'truth'?" She stopped and faced him, defiance making her eyes sparkle. "The 'truth' according to Jack Quinn?"

Refusing to be baited, he stood his ground. "Watch the DVD. Then we'll set up an appointment. I know Drew's in school, but what's your schedule like? Late afternoons or early evenings good for you?"

She turned and headed back in the direction they'd just come. "My work schedule's flexible."

"What do you do? If I know what my client does, I can often find a more relevant way to explain what I'm trying to accomplish."

"I'm an installation artist." She said it as if she didn't expect him to understand what that was.

"Installations. Temporary works? Like those prayer cairns that appeared for a few weeks last summer on Baker Beach?"

She stopped dead in her tracks, her eyes wide. The fog had formed minute droplets in her hair and on her eyelashes, making him think of a land of fairies and sprites and impish spells. She took his breath away.

"D-did you have anything to do with them?" he asked, trying to regain his composure. "The cairns, I mean."

"Yes." For the first time she looked at him with real interest. "You knew what they were?"

"Sure. I've lived in Asia." Though he'd been surprised to see the dozen or so piles of rocks at intervals along the San Francisco coast. They'd appeared as if by magic. Sticks anchored in the rocks bore pennants—scraps of cloth really—on which were written prayers, poems, quotations. There was nothing to explain them, but many people who saw them added to them. "I even tied on a few thoughts of my own. I liked the idea of good vibrations being swept across the entire country on the wind."

Her expression was nothing short of dumbfounded.

"Although I work with animals," he said, "I don't live in a cave."

For a fleeting moment, she seemed embarrassed. Or guilty. "Most people's first thought when they hear *installation art* is dying a river green on St. Patrick's day."

"What do you tell people like that?"

"I tell them, no, it's more like getting the sea lions to lounge in the sun on Pier 39," she said, her tone biting.

"I would think that's performance art," he replied, unable to resist the urge to needle her a little.

"You know the difference?"

"It's not a hard distinction to make. But I do have an aunt who's an art historian. You need to cut most people more slack, though. It's not as if your occupation's an easy one to grasp at first."

She stared hard at him as if she didn't quite know how to take him.

"Do you have anything around the city now?" he asked.

"Actually, I do. The owner of Tryst, the new restaurant in SOMA, asked me for a sidewalk installation. He wanted someone dining inside a Plexiglas cubicle, twenty-four/seven. I told him with a name like Tryst, his restaurant deserved something more subtle. More mysterious."

"So what did you come up with?"

"A visual novella, so to speak. I used the

cubicle and put a table and two chairs inside." As she spoke, an unabashed enthusiasm lit her features, clearing away all wariness. "The next day a glass of wine and a woman's handbag appeared at one place. The day after that, a second glass of wine and a man's umbrella hooked over the other chair. Yesterday some grainy photos appeared thrown on the table. Looked like a private eye might have taken them with a telephoto lens. A man and woman caught in the act. Tomorrow the butt of a revolver will appear from the woman's handbag. The man's chair will be tipped over. Tuesday police tape will appear around the cubicle. And by Wednesday, the whole thing will have disappeared."

He laughed aloud.

"I am having fun with that one although I have to make the changes in the dead of night."

"Alone?" He suddenly felt protective.

"No. There's no shortage of art students in the area who help me on a project by project basis." She suddenly grew distant, as if she'd shared too much. "So…now you know something about what I do, how do you propose

to translate what you do into my language?"
Challenge underlined her every word.

"I don't know. Yet." He took a chance with
a smile. "You might be my toughest case."

"Tougher than the spitz?"

"Yeah. I can't muzzle you."

Her mouth dropped open, then she
walloped him on the arm as his brother had
many times when they were kids fooling
around. Amazingly, the tension between
them eased.

"So you'll watch the DVD with Drew?" he
asked.

"We'll see." She started back toward her
apartment.

What did it take to get her to promise—or
even agree—to anything?

When he caught up to her, she seemed to
make an effort to stay a half step ahead.
Heaven forbid he should lead in any way.
Headstrong woman. But there was a slight
upturn to her mouth, a relaxation in her
shoulders. He sensed she didn't dislike him
quite as much as she had before.

Progress.

As he followed her back to her apartment

and his truck, he thought that, in the brief discussion of her work, he might have discovered a chink in that fortress wall she'd built around herself. The glimpse of the interior didn't reveal dark neuroses or unclaimed baggage, but a clear, strong light that highlighted this woman's need for self-expression and the pride she took in the results. He liked what he saw. A lot.

AFTER A DISCONCERTING Monday morning meeting with Drew's teachers—apparently the mention of bullying got you a school interview as quickly as the mention of chest pains put you at the head of the line in the emergency room—Selena needed a dose of Margo's Bistro. And lunch. She was starving. As was everyone else in SOMA it seemed. There wasn't an empty table in the café. It was so busy Margo and Robert were trapped behind the counter, and their two servers were set on fast-forward.

Resigning herself to take-out, Selena suddenly heard her name called. "Over here!" Derrick waved from a corner table where he sat with Bailey. "Join us!"

"Oh, yes!" The comfort of friends.

Derrick was a contract lawyer and former single dad. He was the only male regular in their inner circle, but he'd been man enough to admit he didn't have a clue about how to raise his two daughters. Until Bailey.

Having made her way through the crowded room, Selena plopped into the chair Derrick pulled out. "Why don't we ever see you anymore?" he asked. Directness had always been one of Derrick's many admirable traits.

"You're seeing me right now. That's one of the reasons I love Margo's Bistro. It provides a public service in reuniting lost friends."

"You know what I mean." He and she had been friends before he hooked up with Bailey. "You haven't come around our place since the wedding."

"Geez, I thought I'd give you guys some privacy." That wasn't it, however. Things had changed. Derrick's priorities—his focus— had changed, and rightfully so. Bailey and the girls were his world. Selena felt uncomfortable intruding. "So, how come you're both here in the middle of a Monday?" she asked.

"Oh, I had errands in the city," Bailey

replied, a twinkle in her eyes, "and I thought I'd meet my hubby for…lunch."

Selena didn't know why they were at Margo's. By the glow on both their faces, they looked as if they'd already had "lunch" at the Marriott.

A server appeared, a new one Selena didn't recognize. The café was such a revolving door of part-time and temporary college help Margo should apply for intern program status. "The special of the day—"

"I'll take it," Selena cut in. "I'm ravenous and whatever Margo makes is terrific. How about you two?"

"We already ordered," Derrick said as the server disappeared. "So why are you here?"

"I don't want to take up your time with my kid problems."

"Excuse me?" Bailey feigned disbelief. "When we're at Margo's the official language is Kid. Spill it."

It was as if someone had popped the top of a shaken soft drink. Selena caught them up on Axel and Sam and Quinn and Drew and the appointment this morning.

"Middle school is cruel," Derrick said. He

should know. His oldest was at that between stage, too. "Is Drew being bullied? What did his teachers say?"

"They said the school has a zero-tolerance policy and a student-teacher-parent conflict resolution committee to handle problems. Drew's never brought an issue before the committee, but his teachers say he isn't very assertive. They say he hovers at the fringes of all the groups. He doesn't seem to have found his niche yet. Lord knows the arts department saved me in school."

"Football, here," Derrick said.

"Academics for me," Bailey added. "But that was high school. Drew's not there yet."

"No, and it's tough being a seventh grader who looks like a sixth grader. Even his teachers noted he's small for his age and quiet. That in itself has made him, on occasion, a target of teasing, some jostling. Some adolescent ostracism in the cafeteria. Not overt bullying, but unpleasant and potentially damaging nonetheless...." Her eyes welled up, stopping the flood of words.

Bailey reached across the table to lay her hand atop Selena's.

"His teachers told me…" This wasn't easy. This was her baby. "To…to try to get Drew to open up. I've tried. But he's shutting me out. They suggested I get him into a group extracurricular activity to build his self-esteem and encourage social skills. How could I have raised a child with low self-esteem?"

"It's the age," Derrick said comfortingly. He grinned. "Plus San Francisco. I just read a great quote. Something about the city dwellers having an existential angst that comes from straddling a fault line."

Selena laughed despite her pain. "You're good friends," she said, dabbing at her eyes with a napkin.

"Hey, we've been there," Bailey said. "And with kids, you know we'll be there again. And again and again and again. You'll be there for us."

Derrick turned serious. "Maybe working with this Quinn guy would be helpful. Male role model and all."

"Oh, please." Selena was just starting to feel better. She didn't need to find out the light at the end of the tunnel was a locomotive. "He's opinionated and unbending. In a word, insufferable. Not qualities conducive to letting Drew shine."

"But if he knows what he's doing with dogs, if he really can get Drew to control Axel, think how good Drew will feel. About himself."

Selena looked squarely at Derrick. "What do you know about dogs?"

Derrick threw his hands in the air. "In a word? Zip. Call this guy."

Realization dawned on Bailey's face. "I think Drew's not the only one with issues here. What really gives, Selena? Is this man, perhaps, attractive?"

"Only if you're a dog. And don't say it."

"Come on. What does he look like?"

"I didn't notice. His alpha-male personality obscured any other impression he could have made. I think he has a head—very large, I can tell you—two arms, two legs. More than that, who knows?"

"I don't believe you." Bailey nudged Derrick under the table. "I suspect you find him attractive, but I also think, if he's as strong-willed as you say he is, you know you couldn't wrap him around your little finger the way you do all the guys you choose to date. And that's what bothers you."

"I liked it better when we were focused on Drew."

Their lunches arrived just in time to interrupt this nasty detour. "So, how are the girls?" Selena asked in an attempt to refocus the conversation.

"Great!" Derrick said, tucking into his lunch.

"We've discovered the trick to keeping a twelve-year-old girl out of trouble," Bailey added. "Keep her so busy she barely has time to breathe. Leslie's trying out for the premier softball league, and we're encouraging it even though it has a more rigorous schedule than the regular league. Anything to burn off preteen angst. And Savannah's suddenly crazy for junior ballroom dancing, can you believe it?"

"How do you juggle work, school—" Bailey had just recently enrolled in a local business college "—and the girls' activities?" Selena asked.

Derrick grinned. "We tag-team."

There it was again. That pairs thing.

"Hey, speaking of teams," Derrick added,

"did you hear Robert wants to get a Margo's Bistro softball team going this season? There's a sign-up sheet at the counter."

Maybe she'd join. Sometimes the solution to life's little aggravations was to whack something.

Driving the short distance home, Selena admitted to herself her friends had come close to being right on two counts. Drew probably would benefit from a mastery of Axel, who outweighed him. And, although she didn't want to waste time and energy exploring this troubling fact beyond acknowledging its existence, a very, very, very—did she mention very?—tiny part of her did find Jack Quinn attractive. But the truth didn't make it any easier to take the next step. To entrust her dog, let alone her son, to Quinn's regimented course of action.

She'd told Sam and the Animal Control officer they'd consulted a dog behaviorist, and that had assuaged the greengrocer's rage. But she didn't tell him Quinn hadn't actually worked with Axel. If Axel's behavior didn't improve, Sam and the rest of her neighbors weren't going to stay mollified.

But, oh, how Quinn had looked at her yesterday. As they'd walked in the intimacy of the fog, he looked as if, at any moment, he could have eaten her up. And she'd felt strong enough to resist until he'd told her he'd seen one of her installations. And he'd gotten it. He knew what it was. He even knew how he was supposed to interact with it without being told. A man that perceptive could prove dangerous.

Dangerous even without the addition of a hard body, a luxurious head of dark wavy hair and chiseled features. Not that she'd noticed what he looked like.

She was prevented from dwelling on the unnerving Mr. Quinn by the necessity of searching out a parking space. Even though her Honda Element was compact enough for even the most challenging San Francisco parking situation, she had to drive around before finally finding a spot two blocks from her loft. It might be time—she'd have to massage the budget—to look for a garage to rent. As she passed Nikki's tattoo parlor, she heard her name. Again. This time the tone was different. Trouble loomed, for sure.

Nikki came running out of her shop. "Babe, you know I love you, but we have a problem."

Now what? Drew was in school. Axel was in the apartment.

The body artist moved to the curb where her vintage Cadillac was parked in a space nobody else in the neighborhood ever—*ever*—used if they knew what was good for them. Lovingly, Nikki ran a hand adorned with Celtic runes over the Caddy's right fender. Selena thought she saw scratch marks. Her heart sank.

"Maxine came by your place," Nikki said. "Axel escaped."

"Oh, no!"

"Don't worry, we caught him," Nikki replied, still caressing the car's custom baby blue finish. "But not before he did this."

Selena tried to think if her car insurance had any clause that would remotely cover Axel damage.

"I talked to Sanchez up the street," Nikki continued. "He thinks he can buff it out. And he owes me. But if it needs a paint job—"

"I'll pay." There went any prospect of a garage in the near future. "You know I'm good for it."

"I know you are, babe." Nikki was toughness itself, but her words weren't unkind. "But you gotta see to that mutt. Before something happens to someone who doesn't love you."

"I will," Selena promised for the second time in only four days.

She knew how critical the situation was, but did Drew? Enough to put Axel in Quinn's hands? Perhaps the very guy who pushed both their buttons was the one who'd already provided a nonthreatening opening. The DVD he'd brought over yesterday. On dog behavior. The one she'd put on the top of the bookcase and promptly forgotten. Maybe it was time to break out the popcorn for an after-school special. She loved Axel's exuberance. She just couldn't afford it anymore.

CHAPTER FOUR

"Did Selena Milano call to make her third appointment?" Jack asked.

Andy looked up from the computer in the trailer office where he was doing his phone-and-scheduling turn in the rotation. "Not since the last time you asked. Fifteen minutes ago. Why does this particular woman make you nervous?"

Andy had to be pulling his leg, although it was hard to tell. Jack did extensive background checks on his employees and interns. He paid well. He created an excellent work environment. But he didn't befriend the staff. Right from the start, however, Andy bent that unspoken rule, whether with personal comments or questions like the one he'd just asked. Outgoing himself, he didn't seem content, leaving Jack to the sole company of animals.

"The only reason I'm asking," Jack explained, "is that I want to make sure you tell her—if she calls—she gets an additional session. The way things worked out, the others barely amounted to one."

"Are you counting Sunday when you made a special trip to deliver that DVD?"

"I thought if her son saw it—"

"Relax, boss." Andy grinned. "I'm riding you. You don't have to explain yourself to me."

Apparently he did.

"If she calls," Andy continued, "how about I let you handle it?"

"No. I have a workshop with the interns this morning. I'll be busy."

"Do you even think she'll call? Her kid was pretty bent out of shape."

"I don't know." He'd delivered the documentary the day before yesterday. Plenty of time for them to watch it. Plenty of time for her to respond.

"Why don't you call her?"

The question was simple, the answer complicated. Complicated by how beautiful she looked veiled in fog. In how she challenged him at every turn, then tempted him to quit his solitary ways. In light of the complications, he decided on his standard professional answer. "I can't help the dog if the owner isn't fully committed to the process."

"While I was giving them the tour, she seemed open."

But her son hadn't been, and he was the key.

Jack remembered his own boyhood. His birth father had run out on them after Jack had been born and returned only to get his mother pregnant with his younger brother. When he was ten, his mother remarried a man who was decent enough but distant. He didn't want to adopt two older boys. Jack watched helplessly as his mother's focus turned to her new husband. As an adult, he now recognized survival instincts. As a child he felt abandoned.

He barely knew Drew Milano, but he didn't want to enter the adolescent's world as a rival.

The phone rang, jarring him out of his thoughts. Andy answered, then immediately handed over the receiver.

"Yes?" He knew who it was before she spoke, and, despite his dark thoughts of only seconds ago, he was glad.

"This is Selena Milano. We watched your DVD, and…you were right…." Her voice trailed off.

"I'm sorry." He couldn't resist. "I didn't catch that."

"You…were…right." She sighed deeply as if the admission had cost her. "Drew became interested instantly. The trouble was he had a million questions. Questions I didn't have a clue how to answer."

"That's what I'm here for."

"That's…what I told Drew."

He found himself inordinately pleased. Found Andy watching. Pleased, as well, it seemed.

"So," she said, "what's next?"

He tried for a neutral tone of voice. "We take Axel to the park."

"Thank goodness! He was getting a complex. Thought you didn't recognize he's actually the dog in the family."

"How soon do you want to meet?"

"I think we should strike while the iron's

hot. Drew's willing, and Axel hasn't damaged anyone else's property in the last twenty-four hours. How soon can you make it?"

"Today after school? Say four?"

"You can get away that quickly?"

"Sure. That's why I have staff." And his staff—it would have to be inquisitive Andy on duty—would have to reschedule two of his appointments that he knew of.

"Then we'll meet in the park near my loft?"

"No. I'll come to your apartment. You need to learn how to take the first step through the door with Axel."

"Good grief, Quinn. There you go with the weird ritual just when I was starting to think you might not be from another planet."

"You're going to thank me after I get done showing you those weird rituals. And the name's Jack."

"Down, boy. I don't know you that well." She hung up.

Leaving him with the receiver to his ear and the sensation the queen had granted him an audience.

If he wanted to keep his head, he'd have to tread carefully in her court. And Andy was wrong. Selena didn't make him nervous. She made him feel alive.

ALTHOUGH DREW didn't seem all that eager about Quinn's visit, Selena found herself unaccountably so. She even managed to find a clean sweater and put on a little lipstick. So she experienced the teensiest bit of disappointment when the dog handler persona arrived, rather than the red-blooded man, and immediately directed his attention toward her son.

Especially since the dog handler looked so damned hot today. Dressed casually, his dark hair tousled over a strong forehead, high cheekbones emphasizing the sculpted quality of his face—making her think portraiture might be a nice line of work—and a four o'clock shadow shading his jawline, making him look as if he'd just stepped out of an outbacking catalog.

"Right now," Quinn said, his deep voice jolting her out of her ill-advised reverie, "Axel runs the house. You and your mom follow his lead. By the time we come back from the park, he's going to see the humans as leaders. And he's going to be a lot happier."

"If you say so," Drew replied, his enthusiasm underwhelming.

"Don't take my word for it. Where's the leash?"

Drew no sooner produced the new one than Axel began to jump and bark.

"He needs to be calm before he steps foot out the door," Quinn said, never raising his voice as he took the restraint.

Good luck, thought Selena.

But as before, Quinn reached out and quickly put Axel in a sitting position, silencing his barking with a sharp, "Hut!" He clipped on the leash, then looked at Drew. "Every day you're going to practice this until the day you get the leash, and Axel automatically responds by taking a sitting position next to the door."

"Shouldn't he, at least, give a command like 'sit'?" Selena asked, feeling a bit left out. "So Axel understands what you want him to do."

"He can," Quinn replied, his tone cool, his eyes devoid of the intense regard he'd held her in the other day. Had she imagined the chemistry between them? "As long as he keeps it consistent. But it's not necessary. Dogs don't talk to each other. They communicate with body language."

"I'm not a dog," Drew said.

"But you're going to be Axel's pack leader. Then all other humans will be pack leader by association."

Axel, still going for the sitting record, looked up at Quinn in rapt attention.

Selena had to admit he was a man to make you take notice. It wasn't his looks so much— although he was ruggedly handsome—as his presence. She'd noticed before that he dominated any space he stepped into. It wasn't an easy task to make her loft seem small, but, somehow, this guy managed to do just that.

"To that end," Quinn continued, "whoever goes through the door first is the undisputed pack leader."

"Axel always runs out ahead."

"I rest my case. But the leadership's going to change today." With the leash tightened, Quinn reached for the door. Axel leapt up. Patiently, Quinn put him back into a sitting position. Axel whined. Quinn gave that odd little, "Hut!"

"What are you saying to him?" Selena asked, curiosity getting the better of her.

"It's just an attention-getter. A warning. Some people growl. Some snap their fingers. Others say, 'Stop!' It doesn't matter. What matters is getting the dog's attention. And consistency."

Obviously. Axel sat awaiting the master's orders. He could be the mascot for a major record label.

As quickly as he'd answered her question, Quinn refocused on Drew. The man was nothing today if not detached and business-like. Had she lost her ability to retain a guy's attention? Or, more likely, was this particular guy more machine than flesh and blood?

After several attempts to open the door and several repetitions of the sit-game, Quinn finally opened the door and Axel... sat. Waiting.

"Wow!" Drew breathed.

"Ditto." Selena was impressed in spite of herself.

Quinn stepped through the open doorway

first, and Axel followed. On the landing he made the dog sit again as Drew and Selena came out, closing the door behind them. Then Quinn led them all downstairs to the sidewalk. A regular pied piper.

Outside he had Axel sit again. "I want you to look across the street." He nodded toward Charlie, shuffling from trash bin to trash bin, Pip tied next to him with a length of insubstantial twine. "It's been my experience the homeless are usually good pack leaders."

Selena looked at Quinn as if he were crazy.

"Contrary to what most people think, the homeless take care of their animals' needs first. Cowboy fashion. And their lifestyle's more like that of dogs in packs. They're always on the move. Migrating, so to speak. Moreover, the human doesn't want to draw attention to himself, so he makes sure the dog behaves. Follows his lead. The whole process feels natural to a dog. Not like the lives of most pampered pets. Where lack of focus and boredom make them act out."

Thank you for that sociology lesson, oh,

Grand Canine Poobah. Selena wondered if this guy really took himself seriously.

"How often do you walk Axel?" Quinn asked, still addressing Drew.

"Once a day."

"When you first get up?"

Selena sensed a trap somewhere in this seemingly simple question. "When he first gets up on weekdays," she interjected, trying to avoid having the two of them look like bad owners, which they were not, "Drew has to get ready for school. So I take Axel outside to do his business, then Drew takes him for a good long run when he gets home."

"Two issues here," Quinn replied evenly. "In the morning Axel's well-rested. Leaving a dog full of physical energy in the house for the day guarantees the dog will find something to destroy. And a run is not the same thing as a controlled walk."

"You're saying someone's going to have to *walk* this dog first thing in the morning?"

"Right after you get up. Every day. Then again in the afternoon."

"I'll do it afternoons, Mom, then twice on the weekends."

"That leaves you with morning duty during the week," Quinn said to her as if that were that.

She didn't like being handed an assignment, unconsulted. No. Given a direct order. From some guy she'd met a week ago. She had to make a conscious effort not to grind her teeth. "This is nonnegotiable?"

"It is if you ever want to have intact sofa cushions."

Damn, he'd noticed her ratty cushions.

He began to walk, dismissing her and immediately bringing Axel to heel. When he spoke, it was to Drew. "The behavioral reason for making a dog heel is that in the dog world—a pack oriented world—the leader leads and the followers follow. You want to be the leader. Sounds simple, doesn't it?"

"Yeah, just like Charlie and Pip," Drew replied, looking as if he was starting to buy into this stuff. "And like in the documentary, too."

Selena trotted alongside, unheeded.

Every time Axel made a move to sniff, stray or explore, Quinn brought him back to attention with a small, quick tug of the shortened leash.

"He doesn't look as if he's having as much fun as Pip," she muttered under her breath.

"Today he's learning," Quinn replied, glancing at her. The man must have canine hearing. "But look at his ears. They're relaxed. Look at his tail. At a calm, submissive half-mast. You can have fun with him in the park. Right now he has to maneuver the people and businesses on the block. On the pack leader's terms. He has to learn his place in the social structure. Besides, Axel's getting a sense of satisfaction—a dog's sense of satisfaction—from following."

So, too, were the shop owners getting a real sense of satisfaction, following the little drama unfolding. The mighty Quinn bringing not only Axel but his two humans to heel. You could tell the neighbors' pleasure by the shared glances and the smirks on their faces. They'd waited a long time for this moment. She should charge an entertainment fee.

"Okay, Drew," Quinn said, "walk next to me. On the other side of Axel. I'm going to hand off the leash to you."

"I don't think I—"

"Of course you can. Get in step. Head and chest high. Arms relaxed. Here we go."

As Quinn, Drew and Axel walked abreast on the sidewalk, Selena was squeezed out of the group and had to drop back a few paces. In the unaccustomed position of follower. When Quinn handed the leash to Drew and the three continued on, Axel in control between man and boy, she felt a sharp pang. The same pang she'd felt when Drew, as a very young boy, had finally gotten the hang of riding a two-wheeled bike. When he'd pedaled beyond her grasp and had kept going. On his own. Without looking back. There was pride in his accomplishment, of course, but a little melancholy, too, at the reminder that children were only ever on loan.

This time the pang was even sharper. She hadn't been the one to guide Drew into his new victory. Quinn, a stranger, had been. Sharing her son—except with Maxine and his teachers, and even that had been difficult at times—had never been an issue before. She'd never let anyone close enough.

She hastened to catch up as Quinn, Drew

and Axel waited for the light at the corner, about to cross the street into the park.

"Mom, this is so cool! Jack says, if Axel and I practice every day, he'll show us some extra stuff. Like how we can in-line skate together."

Despite her son's heartening show of enthusiasm, Selena thought of the cost of those two dance students' lessons, of Sam's bruised fruit, of the Animal Control ticket and of Nikki's scratched car. And of sharing her son. How did you measure the cost of that? "Honey, this is our third session. Right now our budget can't handle more."

"Jack explained we get another session 'cause we kinda had a rough start."

She looked at Quinn.

"Fair's fair," he said with a return of some of the underlying intensity she'd felt on the earlier encounters. His statement might be simple enough, but the hint of question in his eyes unsettled her. What was he asking of her?

The traffic light changed, snapping the tenuous connection, and they crossed the street, the males clearly a solid pack and she...what?

When Quinn made no effort to include her, she sat on a bench. It was the rarest of February days when a little pale sunshine actually made it to the ground. With no point in the city more than four miles from water, the weather was always moist and unpredictable. But with the Twin Peaks to the west of the Mission District absorbing some of the Pacific currents, her neighborhood soaked up more sun and more warmth than any other part of town.

A section of the *Chronicle* lay abandoned on the end of the bench. She picked it up and pretended to read as Drew walked Axel farther into the park with Quinn by his side in serious conversation. There was something about the dog handler, something that went beyond the length of his legs and the sexy taut fit of his jeans. Something she found fascinating at the same time she found repellant. A guilty pleasure. Like a whole bag of Oreos consumed in the middle of the night. Good going down, but heartburn in the making.

She'd resisted the man. She'd complained about him. But, at the same time, she was drawn to him. To his self-assurance. To his quiet but obvious strength. The fact that he now seemed quite unaware of her spiced the mix. She knew she was attractive to men. She dated regularly although she always broke off the relationships before they could get serious. She truly liked her life just as it was, but she might not mind mixing things up a bit by getting to know a man like Quinn. Actually, getting to know him might be too much involvement. Too dangerous. A physical relationship, if they could keep it light and open-ended, might be better—

With a startling flutter of wings, a pigeon tried to land on her paper. Witless bird. She shooed it away. But at least it interrupted a train of thought that was definitely headed toward Looneyville. She needed to get a grip.

Jack looked up from Drew and Axel to see Selena flapping her arms from her seat on the far bench. The woman was a perpetual motion machine. When Drew shot him a questioning glance, he returned his attention to her son. Although his plan of focusing on the dog's needs, on the boy's needs, seemed to be working—Drew definitely had dropped the hostility—he still needed to be careful.

He wasn't about to compromise this kid's feelings for any he himself might have for the mother. No matter how intriguing she was.

"You're doing great," he said to Drew. "Do you think you're ready to have Axel meet other dogs?" He pointed to a woman approaching with a laid-back Lab.

"Axel's gonna wanna jump."

"Not if you're pack leader. Do you know how to meet a new dog?"

"Yeah. Andy said. No eye contact. No touching. No talking until the dog's done sniffing."

"You're a quick learner."

Drew seemed pleased with the simple praise.

"Put Axel in a sit position."

As the woman came nearer, Jack went out to meet her, to ask her if she wouldn't mind being a guinea pig of sorts in Axel's socialization. She agreed. And, as she approached, Drew kept Axel a perfect gentleman. So much so both dogs lay down and snoozed as the humans conversed. That victory led to others as Jack led his students to meet other dogs and their owners, even a tiny, yappy purse-dog on a rhinestone leash. At the first signs Axel might succumb to the other dog's hyperactivity, Drew clicked the leash, bringing Axel back into a calm submissive zone. The boy was in control. The owner of the other dog even commented on the remarkable behavior.

When the three were alone again, Drew boasted, "I could have taught them a thing or two." There was a real sense of accomplishment in his voice.

Kids were a little like dogs in that they seemed quick to return to the joy of the moment. Even though he didn't have kids of his own, it didn't mean Jack couldn't get a small dose of vicarious energy from this young man's achievement.

"You've done really well," he said. "Now, don't get cocky. There may be circumstances where Axel's going to need a little more intense coaching. But I'm not going to show you now, when he doesn't need it. It would confuse him. We'll definitely talk about it next time, though."

"And the in-line skating? We'll talk about that?"

"We'll do more than talk. Have your skates ready." They turned to walk back across the park toward Selena. "Axel's a good dog. With a good disposition. But he's a high-energy dog. That's why you have to walk him every day and make him focus and heel. Running with you while you in-line skate will burn off even more energy. He's also a good candidate to carry a utility pack or participate in agility exercises."

"Awesome!" Drew hesitated. "And we thought you were gonna break his spirit."

"I'm sorry you thought that."

There was a lot he could teach Drew, a lot he could offer. But if he wasn't going to be in it for the long haul, it would be better not to get too close. Not to confuse the boy. Because of his age, Drew was going through biological upheaval as it was. He needed as much stability as the adults around him could muster. He didn't need a man—a potential role model—who was there one minute and gone the next.

Jack had learned that lesson from hard experience.

He now looked at Selena perched expectantly on the bench as Drew and Axel ran to meet her. She might be a woman worth sticking around for. But she'd shown no signs she wanted any kind of relationship. Perhaps because she was already involved in one? The thought gave him pause and a twinge of disappointment.

As Selena listened to Drew rattle on with uncharacteristic fervor about his experience with Axel in the park, she noticed Quinn holding back. Drew's success was the result of Quinn's expertise, but the man was letting her boy bask in all the glory. Damn him for being that big.

"And when we get together again, we're going to take training to the next level," Drew said, sounding so mature Selena had to keep herself from chuckling. Axel sat calmly at Drew's feet. A new dog.

"In-line skating, utility packs and agility courses are one thing," Quinn said, stepping forward, "but the next level at the moment is getting Axel back to your apartment. Through your neighborhood. Without incident."

"Uh-oh." Drew suddenly didn't look as self-confident as he did seconds ago.

"I don't want to hear, 'Uh-oh.' You can do it. Anything that catches Axel's attention, treat it like meeting those dogs and owners earlier."

"You're going to be next to me, right?" Drew looked at Quinn, not Selena.

"Yes. Let's go."

And off they started. The three of them. Without her. Again.

She should be miffed. A part of her was. But there was always something about Quinn that turned displeasure to grudging admiration. This time it was that the man seemed totally comfortable in her neighborhood. Unlike some of the sponsors she worked with on her installations. Unlike many of her dates.

She'd grown up in the blue-collar Mission District when it was mostly Irish and Italian. Now largely Latino, the district was hip and gritty, a vibrant melting pot of machine shops, mom-and-pop stores, chic cafés, thrift stores, artists' lofts and Mexican cafeterias. Not as hilly as other areas of San Francisco, the streets had fairly short blocks, pleasant for walking. Selena loved it for its neighborly atmosphere, but some outsiders thought it not hip enough while others thought it too gritty. Even her friends occasionally expressed concern for her safety.

Quinn, however, seemed unfazed. But when did he ever not? She'd thought of him as controlling. A bit military. But that really didn't describe him accurately. He was more…self-contained. Perhaps it was that untouchable quality that challenged her. She—personally, as well as her art—always got a reaction. But not from him. He seemed to take her, her art and her neighborhood in stride.

As she approached her building, she couldn't believe her eyes. Quinn and Drew stood talking—laughing easily—with Sam as Axel lay at Drew's feet. She should think of a suitable thank-you for this remarkable turnabout. But perhaps the fact that she hadn't been able to rattle the stoic Mr. Quinn was the real reason she took the next, rash step.

"Quinn," she said, calling him away from his conversation.

"It's Jack," he replied, stepping boldly into her personal space and holding her gaze.

She ignored his correction. "Would you

like to come to dinner on Friday? Here at the loft. I'm making *cioppino*."

"I'd like that," he said a little too quickly for her comfort. But hadn't she wanted a reaction?

"Like what?" Drew came up behind Quinn.

"Your mother's asked me to dinner on Friday."

"Just the two of you?" An edge crept into her son's voice. "A date?"

"No!" Maybe she hadn't thought this through. "All of us. Axel, too. It would be an opportunity for Quinn to show us how to handle Axel in his home environment. The park is one thing, but the shopkeepers and neighbors are the ones who've complained. Not to mention our sofa cushions."

A worried shadow passed over Drew's face. "This wouldn't be the extra session, would it?"

"No." Quinn seemed pretty sure of himself. "If we're going to do in-line skating and the other stuff we talked about, we'll have to meet at my center."

"Then this is just dinner." Drew seemed conflicted.

Quinn shot her a questioning look filled

with not a little heat. A fine dilemma she found herself in, with no one to blame but herself and her foolish injured pride.

"Y-yes," she said at last. "If Quinn doesn't mind."

"Do you think if we sit down together over a meal, you could call me Jack?"

Why couldn't she? Because being on a first-name basis with this man seemed like an initial step on the slippery slope to intimacy.

"We'll work on it," he answered for her with a slight twitch at the corner of his mouth that told her, if she hadn't been before, she was in for trouble now.

CHAPTER FIVE

BOTTLE OF WINE in hand, Jack stood on the landing to Selena's apartment and hesitated before knocking. Once he stepped through that doorway—in a nonprofessional capacity—his relationship with the Milanos was either going to improve remarkably or deteriorate irreparably. There wasn't going to be a middle way. Except with their dog.

Nothing ventured, nothing gained.

He knocked, and was surprised to see Selena open the door. Without benefit of backup barking.

"Hey," she said softly as if she, too, was unsure of this situation. "You didn't happen to see Drew and Axel on your way up?"

"No. Should I have?"

"He's so determined Axel be on his best behavior tonight, he took him for a last-minute walk around the block. Axel's third today."

"How's that working out? The walking."

"Quinn, you know how it's working out, and you just want to hear me admit it. So don't mess with me by asking." She stepped aside. "Don't stand on ceremony, either. Come on in."

He entered the loft—still cluttered beyond all reason. Since the last time he was here a jungle of tarps and PVC pipes had sprouted at the far end, but now the laundry had been removed from the sofa, and a table and three mismatched chairs had miraculously appeared near the bank of floor-to-ceiling windows. A wonderful aroma of *cioppino* enveloped him. Remembering the wine, he offered it up.

"Three-Buck Chuck." Examining Trader Joe's house label, she smiled. "At least you know where to shop. Okay. This is your third time here. You're no longer a guest. I can use help in the kitchen." Holding the wine bottle over her head like a battle standard, she marched off, leaving him no choice but to follow.

The rest of the loft might have been a

shambles, but her kitchen was remarkably spotless and organized. Pots simmered on the stove. On a large central butcher's block, chopped raw vegetables in colorful heaps waited to be added to a big bowl of mixed greens. He could see sourdough bread warming in the oven. On the counter, dishes stood in stacks, waiting to be filled. Who knew Selena had this cozy domestic side?

As she pulled a corkscrew out of a drawer, he lifted the lid of the biggest pot on the stove. Dungeness crabs, shrimp and clams simmered in a rich tomato broth. Heaven.

She slapped his hand. "You're letting the steam out. Make yourself useful by pouring us each a glass of wine. Then toss that salad, please."

It had been a long time since a woman had bossed him around a kitchen. He hadn't realized how much he missed it.

Selena pulled a box of pasta from the cupboard. "Drew likes his *cioppino* served over linguini. At his age carbs are of no concern. You can have yours traditionally straight up if you want."

"You think I'm not a growing boy? I'll

have mine over linguini, too." He poured them each a glass of the red wine, then handed her one. "To what shall we toast?"

Beginnings? The unknown? Possible attraction? Or just the pleasure of a man and a woman alone for a few unguarded moments?

For a nanosecond, she looked as if she might be mulling over the options, same as him, but then the loft door opened.

"We're home!" Drew called. "Axel, sit."

"He wants you to see." Nodding toward the outer room, Selena put down her wineglass to stir the linguini in the pot of boiling water. "I'm fine here. Dinner's in ten, max."

He'd been dismissed.

That was okay. He needed a reminder to take it slow and easy.

He stepped into the big room to see Drew standing next to the door and Axel sitting by his side, panting, but relaxed as if the walk had been a beneficial one. "Hi," Jack said, coming up to Drew and extending his hand. Axel remained seated. "How's it going?"

This time Drew took his hand and shook. A good firm grip. "How do you think?" Grinning, he looked down at his dog.

"I think this is the way you're supposed to greet people." The dog's behavior had improved, yes, but so had the boy's. This was no surprise. Time and time again Jack had seen mastery over their dogs turn owners' lives around.

"We've been practicing," Drew said. "With everyone in the neighborhood. Sam even says I might make a good delivery boy."

"That's where a utility pack for Axel would come in handy. I have an extra one at the center."

"What don't you have at the center?"

This. A place that really feels like home. A family.

"So you think we're ready for our next session?" Drew asked, no trace of the former bored and antagonistic adolescent in his question.

Jack looked at Axel, now dozing at his young master's feet. "You're ready. Shall we check with your mother to see how your schedule looks?"

"We have a family calendar on the fridge." Drew led the way into the kitchen. "I just have school, but Mom has tons of stuff she does. And I'd need her to drive."

"I could pick you up." He realized he'd crossed a line as soon as he uttered the words.

Selena stiffened, salad paddles in midair. "I'd like to observe."

"Of course." He mentally kicked himself. She didn't know who he was. This wasn't a casual date picked from the personals. Just two adults. Instead, he'd suggested she entrust her son to him. He didn't have kids, but he could see red flags going up nonetheless. "We can do weekends or evenings," he amended. "The center has floodlights."

"Can we do it soon, Mom?" Drew pleaded. "The next time we get together with Derrick and Bailey, I want to show Leslie Axel isn't rude and crude."

"Who's Leslie?"

"Twelve-year-old girl," Selena replied quietly, crossing to the sink to tip the cooked linguini into a colander.

Enough said.

"Look on the schedule," she continued, setting out shallow bowls and layering the bottoms with the drained pasta.

"We could do it this Sunday afternoon," Drew replied, a smile lighting his face.

She paused in ladling the *cioppino* over the linguini. "So soon?"

Jack wished there was more enthusiasm in her voice. "Sunday afternoon's fine with me." On Sundays the center wasn't open for business. It would just be him and one other staff member on duty. He hoped Andy wasn't scheduled. Andy was following Jack's progress with Selena almost as closely as he followed the Giants.

"But are we interfering with your plans?" she asked.

"Every Sunday morning I take eight different pack members for a run along the Coastal Trail. Other than that, this week I'd planned to catch up on paperwork. You'd be doing me a favor."

"The trail's cool," Drew said, "but we've never taken Axel after the first time. He ran off and we spent the whole time trying to get him back. Now that he can behave, can we come with you sometime?"

Jack caught a warning glance from Selena. "Let's see how he does on Sunday," he replied. "We'll introduce him to the pack and see how well he fits in."

"All right!" Drew picked up the salad bowl and the bread basket and headed for the table. "Come on, guys! I'm starving!"

Selena put the three bowls of *cioppino* on a tray. "Will you bring our wine?" she asked, her tone crisp.

"Are you okay with all this?"

"How could I not be okay with something that has my son so motivated?"

He wished he could believe her.

Selena didn't wait for Quinn as she followed Drew to the table. Why couldn't she be okay? Really okay. At the moment her son was happy. Their dog was sleeping peacefully by the door. Barring the unforeseen, this promised to be a civilized dinner. For a change. Yet a small part of her resented how easily her son and dog had deferred to this guy. How self-same guy had so rapidly changed her family dynamics. In fact, she might consider Quinn the unforeseen.

"Hey, Mom!" Drew said, shaking her out of her pity party. "Did I tell you I got an e-mail from Berta and Rocco?"

"Berta and Rocco are my parents," she said, feeling as if she had to explain to Quinn. To be polite. As hostess who had no one but herself to blame for this sticky situation. "They're in Indonesia. Helping rebuild after the earthquake." She turned to Drew. "What's the latest?"

"Rocco said he saw a Komodo dragon. Berta says they're still having trouble with the government, but they managed to get another bunch of women making baskets for export. She's gonna send you one. Rocco said he'd have sent me a picture of the Komodo, but he was running too fast in the opposite direction."

"The komodo or Rocco?"

Quinn looked surprised. "Isn't Indonesia considered a trouble spot for travelers?"

"They're not exactly travelers." How to explain her unorthodox family? "They're with an organization called Sisters of the Globe. They travel the world helping women establish self-sustaining cottage industries. The group is apolitical—that's really the toughest part for my parents—but it makes them welcome most everywhere."

"How long have they been doing this?"

"A little over fifteen years. Right after I graduated high school." She tried to make her voice light. Tried to concentrate on dishing out salad, making sure everyone had bread. She was proud of her parents, but there was pain, too, in their almost permanent exit from her life. "Oh, we forgot to bring the wine bottle."

Quinn stopped her from jumping up. "I'll get it."

It was amazing how easy he seemed in her space. How comfortable that might make her feel if she'd only let it.

Drew slurped his linguini. "This is your best yet, Mom!"

"Don't talk with your mouth full. And wait for our guest."

"I'm not a guest, remember? Third visit." Quinn returned with the wine bottle and refilled their glasses. You'd think he was the host. "So tell me about your folks. How often do you see them?"

"As often as the Internet is up and running in Indonesia," Drew replied. "And as often as Rocco can get batteries for his camera."

"My son has a very long-distance, twenty-first century relationship with his grandparents," she said, hoping Quinn wouldn't ask about Drew's paternal grandparents.

"There's always Maxine," Drew added. "She's here and she's pretty old-fashioned."

Quinn looked genuinely interested. "Who's Maxine?"

"My former art teacher. My present assistant. And Drew's surrogate grandmother."

"She has green hair and drives a moped," Drew said, reaching for more bread.

Selena laughed. "You have a funny definition of old-fashioned."

"Hey, the moped's a sixties Vespa she rescued from the junkyard."

"Vintage is a little different." Selena turned to Quinn. "The green hair comes from an inhospitable reaction between a home dye job and daily swims at the Y."

"Oh, that makes it sound much more traditional," Quinn said with a wry smile. "Didn't I see her on the stairs Sunday? For some reason she gave me the thumbs-up sign."

Hell, he'd noticed.

"By the way, you're a fantastic cook."

She blushed. She could usually control that little family trait if she had enough warning. "Th-thank you."

"So, were your parents social activists all the while you were growing up?"

Ah. Back to them. By this time her other dates'—did she just think *date?*—eyes usually glazed over, letting her off the hook. "Sort of."

Drew's eyes widened. "Sort of? Only like the California labor movement, all Central American revolutions, the women's movement, the gay movement. Not to mention a few recall movements. If you wanna walk with Axel and me sometime, I can show you the neighborhood murals they helped paint."

Selena was surprised to hear more words come out of her son's mouth than had come out in the past six months combined. Mature words spoken with pride. Although she'd been honest with him about his grandparents, about their contribution to local activism, she hadn't been sure he'd ever paid much attention. He didn't talk about it, so she'd thought he'd seen it all as so much ancient history. Then again, no adults other than herself had ever included him in conversation about it. Until now. Until Quinn.

Jack didn't understand the shift brought about by discussion of parents. Selena's sudden reticence. Drew's new volubility. He wouldn't press the issue, mostly because he wouldn't want someone grilling him on his family dynamics. Although Selena's family sounded fascinating, he'd take a different tack.

He looked at the far corner of the room. "Any projects in the works I can preview tonight?"

"You're so busted, Quinn." Selena's eyes twinkled. "Right now you're looking at my studio, wondering, 'Is that art over there, or the junk she cleared off the table so we could eat?'"

Drew snorted indelicately.

Jack raised both hands in the air. "Guilty as charged. Which means you'll have to show me what's what."

She gave him a little sideways glance. "So you can better assess my needs? As a dog client?"

He didn't answer. Simply enjoyed the hint of flirtation.

"I have a model on the roof," she added.

"If it's not raining, I'll show you after dinner."

He started a quick prayer to whatever fickle weather gods did duty over San Francisco, asking they cut him a break, but a wet nose in his crotch brought him up short. Axel had awakened, and Drew was about to toss him a chunk of bread.

"Don't feed the dog at the table, son," he said, reflex taking over, then immediately regretted the fatherly tone when Drew's expression darkened.

"You have an awful lot of rules." The adolescent resistance made its reappearance. Jack guessed preteens were a lot like unstable dogs who could go from calm to red-zone in a second without warning.

"Not that many rules where dogs are concerned," he replied, recovering the professional tone the boy had originally responded to. "It's all about consistency." He wanted it understood his command had been directed at Axel's behavior, not Drew's. "Pack leaders do everything first, including eating. If you want to teach Axel some tricks using bread after we're finished—away from the table—that wouldn't confuse him."

Selena seemed to sense the tension. "So do all the dogs in your center dress for dinner, eat with their pinkies raised and consult Emily Post when a question of etiquette arises?"

"Close. Except they consult me." He turned to Drew. "Seriously, they have to wait for their food the way you make Axel wait to go through the door. If you want, you can help me feed them when you come on Sunday."

"I don't know. They're not my dogs."

"Meaning?"

"Maybe they won't pay attention to me."

"They will."

"You think?" The boy's natural love of animals was already overshadowing Jack's earlier misstep.

"You've proven yourself a leader with Axel. My dogs will sense it." He relaxed when he saw Drew's smile and the relieved expression on Selena's face.

"Does anyone have room for fruit and cheese?" she asked, rising to clear the dishes.

"Not that fruit Axel knocked into the street!" Drew protested.

"Good heavens, no! My peeps used that up long ago. I promise this fruit has never touched asphalt."

"Her *peeps?*" As Selena headed for the kitchen, Jack looked to Drew for clarification.

"That's what I call the students who help on her projects. Her peeps. Her posse. Her fan club. Her slaves. They're always hungry, and they never have any money, so they raid our fridge."

"How many are there?"

"Project to project, it depends. There's a waiting list. Guys mostly." Drew made a face. "They think Mom's hot."

"Hot?" Returning with the fruit and cheese, Selena plunked the platter on the table. "Where do you come up with this stuff?"

"From them," Drew replied, popping a grape in his mouth. "I hear 'em talking."

Selena looked as if she might blush again. "They're just college boys."

"Whatever."

"And eat with your mouth closed."

Jack marveled at the openness between mother and son. When he was a kid, if he'd used *hot* and *Mom* in the same sentence, his stepdad would have washed his mouth out with soap.

"I'm going to teach Axel a trick." Grabbing the remaining sourdough bread, Drew looked directly at Jack. "Away from the table." He rose. "I saw it on Letterman. It's called a figure eight. Bet we'll have it ready before you go."

"Dinner and a show. How lucky can I get?"

"You won't think you're lucky if Mom has you carrying junk up to the roof. Like her student slaves."

"No carrying," Selena assured him as she looked out the window. "I see clouds, but also a sliver of moon. If you're really interested in seeing this model, we'd better head topside now."

"I'm serious," Jack said. "Make my Aunt June proud. She's the art historian. Dispel my ignorance."

"You're admitting to ignorance?" She shot him a mock astonished look before heading for the door. "Drew! Don't let Axel near the cheese!"

As they climbed the stairs to the roof, she began to talk about her work. About the sponsors. About the site. About the students interning with her. He heard nothing except the musical quality of her voice. Internalized nothing except her scent—something soft and fleeting and tropical—and the lyrical sway of her body as if she were walking barefoot on a beach somewhere. She had an elemental power he'd always associated more with the animal world than the human, and he felt its undeniable pull.

They stepped onto the roof just as the moon and one star emerged from behind the clouds. Bathed in silvery light, she led him around a large topographical model with what looked like a river of miniature banners stuck in the landscape. The design had a sensuous quality. Like its creator. Selena. Goddess of the moon. Beautiful yet distant. She continued talking, but he was hearing an earlier conversation. The one about her parents. When, for a brief moment, she'd appeared vulnerable.

After the tightly controlled calm of his life, he found he relished her roller-coaster moods. The ride was unpredictable, sure, but exciting.

She cleared her throat. "You aren't paying attention. I have half a mind to call your Aunt June. Tell her you're in danger of flunking Art 101."

Oh, he was paying attention all right. With all his senses. "Will this be on the test?"

"I'll test you." She looked as though she might wallop him again as she'd done on their brief walk in the fog.

Suddenly, beautiful music floated up to the rooftop. Chopin?

"Drew has pretty sophisticated taste," he said.

"This is one of the reasons I love the Mission District," she said. "There's always music of one kind or another playing. It makes me feel my life has a soundtrack."

She led him to the low wall edging the roof, then pointed across the street. In a lighted window above an import shop a young girl sat at a piano, her feet dangling inches above the floor. She played with a seriousness well beyond her years.

"That's Katya," Selena said. "She's eight. Every morning before school it's scales, scales, scales, but every night it's this glorious concert. She's getting ready for her recital. Neither of her parents have ever had any kind of musical training, but they recognize Katya's gift. They've sacrificed for the piano. For her lessons. They're wonderful parents."

"Tell me more about your parents," he said.

She stopped speaking, and looked at him, her emotions unmasked in the moonlight. "What about them?"

"Start with something simple. Were they wonderful parents?"

"You can't begin to understand how far from simple that question is."

"Why?"

"I love them. And they've always loved me."

"But?"

"No buts." She seemed to steel herself.

"Do you miss them?"

"Of course."

"Do you resent that they've spent so much time away?"

She turned to look out over the neighborhood garden of neon below. "They left, assured they didn't have to look back because they'd done what they were supposed to in raising me."

"And what was that?"

"They raised me to be independent. Self-reliant." She tilted her chin as she turned back toward him. The light in the depths of her eyes again flashed a determined invincibility. The queen had returned.

She'd said they'd left fifteen years ago. Drew was twelve. He wondered about Selena's circumstances as a young mother. Had she been married? If so, why didn't it work out? Why wouldn't her parents want to stay and help? Be close to their grandchild?

"What do you remember most about your childhood?" he asked instead.

She took a deep breath, then spoke carefully as if she'd been practicing all her life in case someone asked her this question. "By act and word, my parents constantly reminded me that being one's own boss was the key to surviving in a complicated world. When... when I was little, I'd grab onto my mother's skirts, her jeans. Berta would say, 'Don't cling, dear.' Rocco always reassured me with, 'There's my strong girl.'" She faltered.

Later he would tell himself he only wanted to assure her that everyone needs to lean on someone once in a while.

He wrapped his arms around her and pulled her close.

She responded in a way he thought impossible. By melting into him.

If she'd pulled away, he would have let her. Because it was too soon. For both of them. But she didn't, so he kissed her.

And he didn't hold back.

Selena had been expecting the kiss, but not the tender embrace that came before. As soon as they'd stepped onto the roof and she'd felt the expanse of night above them, she'd felt anything was possible. Especially a kiss. And she'd begun to arm herself against letting it happen. Especially when the music began like the score to some overwrought film. But Quinn hadn't used the moment the way she'd expected. He hadn't put the moves on. Instead, he'd drawn her into talking about her parents. Had made her feel a little-girl pain she knew she had no right to feel. It was his reaction to that pain that proved her undoing. That embrace. Protective. Tender. Too seductive in its tenderness.

And now she felt herself drowning in his kiss.

This wasn't a get-the-girl-in-bed kiss. She'd handled those in the past. No, this kiss was a litmus test to prove if they fit together. At a most elemental level. And, damn, did they fit.

So much so, it frightened her.

She pushed away. "I… I need…space."

He didn't apologize. Or step in to convince her otherwise. He didn't leave in a huff. He didn't move. He let her have the space she claimed she wanted.

"I'm not saying I didn't see that coming," she said, feeling a rush of words begin to tumble out. Oh, please, don't let her sound like an hysteric. "And I'm not saying I didn't enjoy it. I did. Who wouldn't? But…but let's just blame it on the moonlight. And the music. And my most excellent *cioppino*."

She felt a giggle rise in her throat, and

knew she'd gone round the bend for certain. Suppressing the giggle, she hiccuped instead. "I know we're two adults, and—*hic*—a kiss is just a kiss…*hic*. But if you thought—*hic*—I was sending out signals, I wasn't. Some women might find you attractive—I know Maxine does…*hic*—but I can't afford to. I have a twelve-year-old son who is the—*hic*—only permanent man in my life. I have—*hic*—a career. And I'm, by nature, a woman set in her solitary—*hic*—ways. At least where relationships are concerned. Do you under-*hic*-stand?"

"I understand 'space' is often an excuse to avoid meaningful connection. Commitment."

"Then you understand?"

"I do."

"Please, don't think it was the kiss. It wasn't. Specifically. You're a lovely kisser. Really you are." She searched his face for a reaction. Hurt. Irritation. Resignation. But he had complete mastery over any emotions he might be feeling. "And I'm babbling—*hic*."

He didn't disagree.

"So, can I make you a cup of coffee?"

"No, thanks. I have an early day tomorrow. I'd better shove off."

"Drew's going to want you to see that trick."

"I wouldn't miss it."

Okay, now she was confused. She'd just blown him off, but he was willing to stay to see her son perform a stupid pet trick? He was so not like the other guys she dated. Not that this had been a real date.

Downstairs Quinn seemed relaxed. He even snagged some orange slices before she cleared the fruit and cheese platter. How could he eat after that kiss? Her stomach was still in a knot. He laughed—a genuine laugh, not some polite but tense I'll-show-her laugh—as Drew coaxed Axel in a figure eight around his legs. To accommodate the dog's bulk, her son had to stand on tiptoe on one leg and throw the other in the air in a move that would make a cancan dancer envious. He nearly fell several times.

"Hey," Quinn said, "maybe we should run you as well as Axel on the agility course Sunday."

He was still talking Sunday?

At the door he looked her square in the eye and said, "If you ever give up your art, you can open a restaurant. The dinner was great. Thank you."

That was it?

No *I'll call?* No *We'll talk?* Not even *Screw you?*

Who was this guy? And why was he being so freaking weird?

CHAPTER SIX

"I HAVEN'T SEEN you in awhile, so you're going to have to rewind and start from the beginning!" Nora exclaimed, bursting into the bistro where Selena, Margo and Bailey sat, sipping coffee and comparing the relative merits of Keith Urban, Russell Crowe and Heath Ledger. "Where are Derrick and Rosie?"

"Derrick pulled softball practice duty," Bailey replied, "so I get to play with the adults."

"Rosie says her schedule's impossible." Margo stood to get Nora her usual chai latte. "She sneaks away from campaign headquarters every so often to hide out here. Says she'd love it if we'd call a real meeting so she can put it in her PalmPilot and give it official, must-attend status."

"Evenings work best for me," Nora said.

She eagerly rubbed her hands together. "Now, what did I miss?"

"We haven't started dissecting the important stuff," Bailey replied with a mischievous grin. "Selena's date."

"Since when do you consider a date important enough for group discussion?" Nora asked, genuine surprise registering in her question.

Fair enough. In past conversations Selena had always considered men merely for their passing entertainment value. Not fodder for serious discussion. Kids were serious. Jobs were serious. The environment was serious. Not dates. "I first have to clarify," Selena insisted. "He wasn't a date. He's just a guy who's…who's…"

"Who's gotten under Selena's skin," Margo finished for her. "At long last."

"Don't be hard on our girl," Nora cautioned. "You know I never thought I'd love again." Widowed with a young child, Nora had been besieged by survivor's guilt.

"But you were open to the possibility."

And the possibility had shown up in the form of Erik, an orthopedic surgeon at the hospital where Nora worked as a physical therapist. A former Olympic skier and risk-taker, Erik convinced Nora she should risk a second chance. With him. She did, and she hadn't stopped glowing since.

"I'm open to possibilities," Selena protested. "Just not long-term and not with this guy."

"So who is this guy?"

"Her dog handler," Bailey said, licking her finger, then putting it up to her thigh with a, "Ssss!"

Selena laughed. "He is so not hot. Besides, you've never met him."

"Granted, I only have your reaction to go on, but that in itself tells me he's a force to be reckoned with."

Nora looked confused. "You obviously know something I don't know. Back up a bit."

"Jack Quinn is a dog behaviorist," Selena explained. "Called in under duress. But I have to admit he's worked miracles with Axel. To thank him, I invited him to dinner."

"And that's all we know," Margo assured Nora. "So how did it go last night?"

"Dinner?" Nora settled in for a tale. "Where did you take him?"

"He came to my place." This was hard for Selena to make public. Even to her friends. She didn't let men-who-were-not-interns hang out at her place.

"Oh?" Increased interest made Nora's eyes grow wide.

"You're all making way too much of it," Selena said, knowing they weren't. And they hadn't even gotten to the kiss and Quinn's strange behavior afterward. "He has as much to do with my son and my dog as he does with me."

"And Drew doesn't like him? Is that the issue?"

"Drew didn't. At first. Now he thinks Quinn hung the moon."

"But you don't."

"He has his moments," she admitted.

"Okay," Bailey said, "what makes last night worthy of today's discussion?"

"He kissed me." There it was. Out in the open.

"And that's a big deal, why?"

"First of all, it wasn't a kissing kind of

night," she replied, but was that ever a lie. The scene on the rooftop was eminently kiss-worthy. "It was a thanks-for-keeping-my-dog-out-of-the-pound kind of night. Second, I pushed him away."

"For kissing you?" Margo put her hand on Selena's forehead as if feeling for fever. "Delusions of virginity. I hear that's going around."

"Cut her a break," Nora admonished. "We just went to a PG movie that had a romantic kiss. With all the fervor of a true six-year-old Danny shouted, 'Gross!' Right in the crowded theater. So did this guy fall into the gross kisser category?"

"Uh, no. Definitely not. But, actually, the kissing part and the pushing away part aren't the issue."

"What else is there?"

"I told him I needed space."

"Selena's mantra," Nora commented with a knowing nod. "How'd this one react?"

"You could say he didn't. At least he didn't make a big deal out of it. Afterward, he stayed around to see a trick Drew taught Axel. Had a little dessert. Said good night.

And that was that. No cold shoulder. No hurt pride. No posturing. Don't you think he's weird?"

"Because he did what you asked?" Bailey looked at Margo and Nora. "I don't know about you, ladies, but the man sounds dangerous."

"Put that way, my complaint does sound a bit silly," Selena allowed. "But what if he is dangerous? I don't really know the man. Although Robert does. Robert? Would you come here for a minute and clear up a weighty matter?"

Robert came over cautiously. An intelligent man, he knew better than to throw himself under the wheels of this careening estrogen-fueled bus. "If you're going to make me break a tie, I'll have to vote Russell Crowe. Only because I think he's this generation's John Wayne."

"Nice try at evasion," Selena said, "but I'm interested in what you know about Jack Quinn. Any aberrant behavior in his past I should know about?"

"I know his brother from the gym. I met Jack a couple times in passing. They moved to San Francisco when both of them were in high school. Their mother had just divorced their stepfather. A few years later, she moved on to Arizona, I think. Jack and his brother stayed here. They're good people. Beyond that, if you want specifics, you need to ask Jack."

"So you have no idea why he might appear hot for me one minute then frosty as a Sno-Kone the next?"

"I…think I have a customer at the register." Robert made a hasty exit.

"Selena, you do have a way of putting men on the spot," Bailey said with a laugh. "What not-so-subtle question did you drill Jack with that you're not telling us?"

"I've told you everything, but I'm still really puzzled by how easily this guy goes from sixty to zero in no time at all."

"I hate to say it," Margo said, looking for all the world as if she were handling a live grenade, "but maybe he's just not into you. Maybe he thought he could be, but after the kiss…I don't know…lack of chemistry?"

"Oh, there was chemistry!" That she couldn't get her friends to see her dilemma ruffled Selena's feathers no end. "Both organic and physical."

"After which, you told him to back off, and he did." Nora noted. "'Fess up, Selena, what did you really want?"

"Well, maybe if I were honest…it would have been nice if he'd melted into a little adoring pool at my feet."

The three women hooted so loudly everyone in the café turned in their direction.

"All the other guys you date eventually do just that," Margo reminded her. "And you kick them to the curb as soon as they do."

"I'm looking for sympathy, not logic." Selena played with the Danish crumbs on the plate in front of her. "Have you ever run into a guy so impossible you want to—" She leaned forward and shot a warning glare at her friends. "What I'm about to say does *not* go beyond this table." She took a deep breath. "Have you ever wanted to…to throw caution to the wind and run off with this unthinkable person for a long-lost weekend?"

"Uh-huh!" The chorus was immediate and unanimous.

Selena looked at Bailey and saw Derrick. At Margo and saw Robert. At Nora and saw Erik. After initial resistance, they'd run with their impulses. And what had that folly precipitated for all three couples? Commitment. Something Quinn had accused her of avoiding.

Bailey tried to look serious. "So you don't think you're going to see him again?"

"Oh, we're supposed to meet tomorrow at his center."

Three pairs of raised eyebrows met her statement.

"What?" Selena loved these women, but sometimes she felt as if they all knew something—about her—she didn't.

"Is this one of your paid sessions?" Margo asked.

"You see, that's strange, too. Technically, we've had our three sessions. Axel's done a total turnaround. Job complete. But Quinn says he's throwing in another session. To show Drew some extra stuff."

"Let me get this straight," Nora said. "He's won over your dog and your son. He kissed you. He's now throwing in freebies. I'm only going with a gut reaction here, but I think he's interested."

"Then why is he being so damned unflappable about my insisting on a little distance?"

"Maturity?" Bailey offered. "Maybe it's going around, along with delusions of virginity."

Nora threw up her hands. "I've got it. He's a dog handler. Used to taming the untamable. Or, in your case, Selena, the incorrigible. Maybe he has your number, and maybe he already has a strategy for winning you over. He's got to be patient, working with dogs. Maybe he's willing to wait for you. Make you come to him. Maybe... you've met your match."

Could that be?

The thought both terrified and excited Selena.

So much so, she thought of nothing else all afternoon as she and Drew and two of her interns scoured the Scroungers' Center for Reusable Art Parts for cast-off materials for future projects. She found herself listening to the easy—sometimes too easy—guy talk of the interns. She even let herself indulge in a little light flirtation with one of them until she caught Drew making a gagging motion. One thing was clear. Compared to Quinn, the college interns were mere boys. In substance and mental age, closer to Drew. She didn't like that Quinn came out top dog.

She might not like it, but she couldn't get him out of her mind. Even dreamt of him. Dreams that centered around his kiss. A kiss so memorable it covered all the elements on the periodic table and charted a few new ones. When she awoke, she was disturbed to remember the real kiss hadn't packed any less potency. And the girls had questioned the chemistry. Hah!

Sunday morning crawled by, and Selena was beset by the fact that she didn't want to see him again. Because she knew she'd end up trying to explain him to her friends at a future date. Maybe she'd bring her video camera under the guise of taping Drew with Axel. Then she could replay the session at the bistro. And her friends could see the problem for themselves. But would the problem even show up on tape? Was it all in her head? Maybe Margo was right. Maybe Quinn assessed the kiss and determined he just wasn't into her. It was early enough in their relationship-that-wasn't-a-relationship that bailing out wouldn't affect his professional equilibrium.

His demeanor at the dog center did nothing to dispel that notion. Once again, as in the park, he was all business, taking Drew aside to work with Axel. She was relegated to a lawn chair under threatening clouds, with an old paperback she found crammed in the bottom of her backpack, and a hot coffee Andy thoughtfully brought her. Alone with her unanswered questions, she regretted not having brought the video camera. She could have filmed herself for some future project, titled *The Slow but Sure Sabotage of One Woman's Sanity.*

OUT OF THE CORNER of his eye, Jack saw Selena bundled up and reading in the lawn chair. It was the longest he'd ever seen her so still. He didn't want to shut her out, but she'd made it clear she valued her space. Besides, where Axel was concerned, he needed to focus on Drew. Jack knew how difficult it was for a kid to eke out his own space, his own style, his own path in the shadow of a dominant adult personality. While Selena wasn't controlling the way his stepfather had been, there was no denying her presence at any given moment. To find himself, Drew would need to step beyond her shadow. Sole mastery of his dog was a move in the right direction.

So, if Selena wanted space, now was a good time to give it to her. Although, after Friday night—after that kiss—Jack was absolutely certain he couldn't turn his back on her altogether.

"Run him once more through the obstacle course," he called to Drew, "then we'll see how well he socializes with the pack."

Both Drew and Axel had taken to the obstacle course like naturals and had devoted themselves to nothing but since their arrival. There was no reason they shouldn't consider competition if Selena was willing. Another positive outlet for both boy and dog. So absorbed had he been in this new challenge, Drew hadn't even mentioned in-line skating. His skates and helmet lay abandoned on a bench. Maybe they'd have to save that activity for another day. Jack could only hope.

"He's hot," Drew said of Axel as they trotted over after the last obstacle. "I bet he'll go right for one of those pools."

"Even so, before he goes into the free-roaming area, make him sit," Jack said, pleased at the happiness both boy and dog exuded. "Then, when he's calm, lead him through the gate and immediately drop the leash. The dogs will sort everything out on their own. We'll be there just in case they don't."

Without question, Drew did exactly as Jack asked. Trust. It was a beautiful thing, hard won in the human world and not to be treated carelessly. He knew from painful experience. By the time he'd latched the gate and turned around, Axel had flopped on the ground and had shown his underside to the smallest of the pack, who, if Axel were standing, wouldn't come up to his belly.

"Is Axel okay?" Drew asked, concern creeping into his voice.

"Yes. He's giving the dog version of 'I come in peace.'"

And just like that Axel became a part of the pack, with a couple dozen brand-new best buds. No matter how often he saw it, this assimilation gave Jack an immense sense of satisfaction. If only humans could as easily gain acceptance, his brother and he would never have been stuck in outsider roles every single time they were placed in a new school.

"You sure know a lot about dogs," Drew said, his words tinged with awe. "Did your dad teach you?"

"No." The only thing life with his stepdad had taught him was never to expose his own underbelly. "My stepfather didn't allow pets. And I never knew my biological father."

"Me, either."

The boy's quiet admission startled Jack. He glanced over at Selena, who was out of hearing range, and wondered if her son was telling tales out of school.

"It's okay," Drew said, noticing. "Mom's cool with it."

"Are you?"

"I guess you can't miss what you never had, but…"

"But?"

"Sometimes I wonder. What he's like. Do you?"

He had. Until shortly after it became clear his stepdad wasn't going to fill any fatherly void, when he'd asked his mother about his "real" dad. She'd said the man had abandoned them, and then had let loose with such a stream of vitriol Jack had never dared ask again.

"Yes," he replied simply. "I still wonder at times." No need to load the boy with someone else's baggage. "Have you asked your mom about him?"

"Some. She'll talk to me about anything, but I can tell she really doesn't want to talk about him. She always says it just didn't work out."

"Often that's the only answer there is. My mom divorced my stepdad. She couldn't take military life. She still says it just didn't work out."

"But does she talk about him?"

"Once in a while."

"No offense, but he was your stepdad. This is my real father we're talking about, and my mom acts as if it's no big deal. She doesn't even keep a picture of him."

"Maybe because it was a big deal. Maybe

it still hurts her, but she doesn't want it to hurt you. Maybe she thinks if she can't say something good, she won't say anything."

"She did say he was real smart."

Not very if he'd let Selena go.

"Like father, like son," he said instead. "You get an A-plus in dog-handling."

"Thanks." Drew looked down at his feet. "I've been thinking a lot lately…about maybe trying to find him. What do you think?"

He thought they were now venturing onto very thin ice.

"Before you do anything," he cautioned, "talk it over with your mom. Get her to tell you more about your dad. You might change your mind, the more you know. And you need to be careful of her feelings."

"What do you mean?"

"She might take it that you're not happy with your life with her."

"Gosh, that's not it!"

"What is it then? Have you thought it through?"

"It's hard to explain."

"Try me. I've been there."

Drew looked up at him, his eyes wide. "I love my mom, but we're not a lot alike. So I wonder if I'm like…him."

He'd wondered the very thing. In fact, if his own biological father had been the monster his mother had described, what did that make him?

He gave Drew the only answer he'd been able to come up with. "Think of it like this. Maybe we get a little bit from our moms, a little bit from our dads. But the rest of our lives we get to invent ourselves."

"You think?"

"I think it's always better to look forward than backward."

"So you're saying I shouldn't try to find him?"

"I'm saying you need to discuss all this with your mother." It hit Jack he'd discussed his own feelings not with his mom, not with his brother, but only now, with a twelve-year-old he'd met two weeks ago.

"Drew!" Selena's voice nudged him out of introspection. "We need to get going. Maxine's coming over to help put together all the materials for the installation tomorrow."

Drew went to the edge of the dog compound and hung on the fence. "But we didn't even get to in-line skate."

Jack came alongside Drew while Selena met them from the opposite side of the fence.

"Now that you have control of Axel," she said, "I think you can manage skating on your own."

"But what's the fun in that?" Drew shot back. "Jack was going to skate, too, with some of his dogs."

"Really?" Her mouth turned up at one corner.

"Do I not look as if I can skate?" Jack asked.

"You look as if you could do anything you want," she replied. "But I didn't exactly picture you on skates."

"Too old?"

"Perhaps too buttoned-down."

"Mom!" Drew protested. "And you tell me not to be rude!"

"Maybe we need to prove your mother wrong, Drew. Maybe we all need to go skating."

Jack was pleased to see he had the power to surprise Selena. She backpedaled. "I'm not sure I need to get up on skates, too. I was thinking more along the lines of observing."

"I wasn't thinking of a few laps around the compound."

"What did you have in mind?"

"My brother's a fitness nut. And a member of the Midnight Rollers. Kind of installation art on wheels. Ever hear of them?"

"No." But interest flashed in her eyes. He had her.

"They meet every Friday night at nine at Ferry Plaza at the Embarcadero, then they skate a route throughout the city. Sometimes only a couple dozen show up, sometimes a couple hundred. My brother says it's as close to running with a human pack as I'm ever going to get."

"You have a brother who lives in the city?"

"And here I thought you'd given up that idea of me coming from another planet."

She smiled up at him with a look that was half mischief and half come-hither. "Do we get to meet him and see for ourselves if he has antennae?"

"Rule one—everyone has to wear helmets, so his antennae will be hidden, but, believe me, he'll want to meet you. He's been concerned I don't associate enough with humans."

"Yeah, be careful. Central command will recall your mission. It'll be back to the mothership for you, buddy boy."

"And I've just begun to break in this body."

"Can we bring Axel skating?" Drew asked, stepping between the adults.

"I think so," Jack said, tearing his gaze from Selena. "Since it's our first time and we probably wouldn't do the entire route. Axel and some of my dogs could handle up the Embarcadero to Fisherman's Wharf and back. But I'll call my brother and ask if dogs are allowed."

"And if they're not," Selena said, challenge in her voice, "what would the point be?"

"To skate," he replied. "The three of us. Maybe get something to eat. Take Axel to Golden Gate Park another day. How does that sound to you, Drew?"

"I get to skate in the street at night? Awesome!"

"Oh, I never asked you," Jack said, turning to Selena with mock concern. "Can you skate?"

She took the bait. "You're not the only one who can do anything they set their mind to. Call your brother, and be prepared to eat my dust."

Selena couldn't believe Quinn had gone from letting her cool her heels to turning on the charm and getting her to agree to danger on wheels. "Go get Axel, Drew. Maxine's probably waiting."

When she and Quinn were alone, she leaned over the fence. "Did you just talk me in to a date?"

"Believe me, I don't flatter myself into thinking I could talk you into anything." His gaze was intense. Warm. With a hint of laughter in his eyes. "Besides what kind of a date involves a half-dozen dogs and a twelve-year-old kid?"

He had her there. None of the other men in her life had ever given two thoughts to her son.

Drew leashed Axel and brought him around to her side of the fence. "You're going to call your brother about this Friday?" he asked, his question full of a boyish eagerness that had been sadly in short supply until the arrival in their lives of extraterrestrial Quinn and his Dog Star magic.

"Who said anything about this Friday?" she asked.

"Do you have plans?" Quinn asked.

"I might."

"Then check your schedule, and when I get back to you, we can set up a Friday. Any Friday."

"I hope it's this week," Drew said, "and so does Axel. Don't you, boy?"

Axel whined in anticipation. Selena felt like whining for totally different reasons. Nora might have been right. Quinn may have outstrategized her. And the whine? That would be for her failure to object.

In the Honda on the way home, Axel snoozed in the back seat and Drew seemed to retreat.

"Did you have fun today?" she asked. He'd been so animated at the center.

"Why don't you have a picture of my father?" he asked suddenly. "Why don't you tell me stories about him?"

She felt as if she'd been sucker punched.

"Why do you ask about him now?"

"Because Jack and I talked about him today."

Make that a double sucker punch with the

added shock that her family's privacy had been laid bare.

"Why would you talk about him to Quinn, of all people?"

"'Cause Jack said he had a stepdad. He didn't know his real dad. And I said, me, too, and we got talking."

"About?"

"About how we both wondered what they were like. About…maybe looking for them."

She nearly drove off the road.

"Quinn told you to look for your father?" she asked, trying desperately to control her rising anger.

"No! That was my idea. He told me to talk to you first. He told me, if you talked to me about my dad—really talked to me—I might change my mind. But I wouldn't know, would I, if you never say anything about him?"

Drew's father was a painful part of her past. A part she thought she'd closed. Permanently. She didn't want to dredge up the pain and transfer it to her son. She wanted the problem to go away.

And she wanted to hurt Jack Quinn for bringing the problem into the light of day.

˙She managed to stall Drew until they got home by telling him this was a discussion best held face-to-face, not dodging traffic. Maxine wasn't at the loft yet, so there went that possible postponement. Selena made a pot of cocoa.

"I'm not going away," Drew said softly, standing at the edge of the kitchen, "until you tell me everything."

She was surprised he wasn't throwing a preteen tantrum. In fact, she now saw some of Quinn's quiet determination modeled in her child.

"What do you mean by 'everything'?" She poured cocoa into two mugs, then handed Drew one.

He made no move to take the conversation to the couch or anywhere else more comfortable. "Who's my dad? How did you meet? Why aren't you with him? Start at the beginning. Something more than 'it just didn't work out.'"

Suddenly, for the first time, it struck Selena how alone she was in her role as parent. Drew had moved beyond the age when pat answers worked. And here she stood with no spouse to tag team with her. Her parents were halfway around the world. As Drew stared her down, she couldn't even call upon her friends and their advice.

But she could think of the issues the single-with-kids group had faced and discussed and solved. She could draw on their collective wisdom. She'd always been open with Drew—too open, some had said—and had always responded to his questions honestly. She'd wanted to be strong for him. A person who had all the answers. But this new set of questions would show Drew his mother had been young and weak and stupid.

"Mom?"

"Where to begin?" She took a deep breath. "You know I went east to school. The Rhode Island School of Design. There, in my junior year, I—I fell in love with one of my instructors. He was much older." God, this was hard. She looked away from her son's insistent stare. "I became pregnant."

"With me."

"Yes. I dropped out of school. Moved back here. Maxine helped me. That's all there is to tell. Except I never, ever regretted having you." She moved to hug him, but he recoiled.

"Does my father know about me?"

"No."

Drew's eyes suddenly filled with unshed tears. "Why not?"

How could she explain to a twelve-year-old that she'd entered a relationship with this man—this man with a wedding ring on his finger and family photos on his desk—with absolutely no consideration for his wife and kids? Only when faced with pregnancy, had she thought of the woman as a real person with real children—all with very real feelings like her own—and of how their lives could be blindsided. By then, she couldn't bring herself to undo what had been done, and quiet departure seemed the better part of valor.

"He was already married. He had children. He didn't love me." That last had been an enormous blow to her twenty-year-old ego. Now, she felt shame at how self-centered she'd been. "We had no future together."

"But doesn't he deserve to know about me? Don't I deserve to know him?"

"It's not about deserving. It was about what was best for everyone involved. At the time. He could have lost his job—"

Such a look her son gave her. Disbelief? Fear? Scorn? She'd never seen the toxic combination on his face before. His eyes now dry and steely, he turned without comment and headed for his room.

"Please, Drew, come back. Tell me what you want me to say. Tell me what you want to do."

"I don't know," he called over his shoulder, and she could hear the catch in his voice. He slammed the door to his room.

She slumped against the kitchen counter, then felt Axel's cool, moist nose in the palm of one limp hand. Drew had shut out the world, including his mother and his best bud. Axel whined. Selena slipped to the floor and buried her face in the fur of his neck.

CHAPTER SEVEN

HIS BROTHER was coming over, and Jack felt guilty.

When he'd called to ask about the Midnight Rollers, he'd actually hoped to get Ted's voice mail, then let phone tag provide the answer. But, instead, he got his brother in person. As soon as he'd uttered the words, "I have a question," Ted had said, "Save it for face-to-face. I'll be right over with take-out."

It wasn't that Jack didn't love his brother. He did. In fact, he'd spent their childhood protecting Ted. Serving as a father figure as much as a kid could. But after Anneka had died, Jack found it difficult to be around those who should be closest to him. Except for the dogs.

His younger brother, however, had refused to give up on him.

The doorbell rang, and Jack opened the door to Ted loaded down with containers that smelled deliciously of Thai food. "I'm looking for Jack Quinn," he said. "Do you know him?"

"Very funny. Get in here."

"You sound like him," Ted continued, brushing by into the one-room apartment, beginning to unload containers onto the counter that served as both work space and eating area, "but I haven't seen him in three months, so it's hard to tell."

His brother paused and looked about, as if in surprise. "This is the cell I remember, so perhaps you are he." He glanced at the one easy chair in the living space. "Where shall we eat? Standing up here, or standing up on your balcony? Aren't monks allowed furniture for guests?"

Jack pulled two stools from under the counter. He liked the spareness of his home. With a skylight and glass doors to the balcony, it had excellent light. He'd designed the interior with a ship's economy so that storage space flush with the walls held everything out of sight, even his bedding. "It suits me," he said.

"Sadly, it does," Ted agreed, opening containers of spring rolls, pad Thai, crabmeat basil-fried rice and fresh ginger stir-fry. "But what I can't understand is how a guy can disappear—totally disappear—in five hundred square feet of living space." He frowned at the feast. "I forgot beer."

Jack pulled two bottles from his fridge.

"Dig in," Ted said, handing Jack a set of chopsticks. "So what's your question?" All his life, his brother had run nonstop and in high gear from activity to activity and subject to subject. It had driven their stepdad nuts.

"I want to know about the Midnight Rollers. If I come, can I bring dogs?"

Ted paused in slurping a noodle, his expression one of more than passing interest.

"A couple friends and I," Jack continued, "were thinking of bringing maybe a half-dozen dogs."

"Who are the friends?"

"A woman and her son. Former clients."

"Does this woman have a name?"

"Selena Milano. She's an artist in town."

Ted pulled the laptop Jack kept on the counter closer and brought up the Internet.

"What are you doing?"

"I'm Googling Selena Milano. I want to make sure she doesn't do sofa art. If she does, you can't bring her." A big grin crossed his face as images of Selena's work flashed on the screen.

"I take it she's in."

"Look what she's doing this week." Ted turned the screen so Jack could see the artist's rendered proposal. "Down near the ballpark. The block that's being demolished for that condo-shopping-dining complex. She's putting a wind harp on the old frontage. It'll stay up until the wrecking ball comes. She's calling it 'Swan Song.'"

"This afternoon she mentioned she'd be installing a new project this week."

"You saw her this afternoon?"

"The way you hop from one subject to the next," Jack said, "I can't believe you can focus long enough to edit a magazine."

"It's an alternative magazine," Ted retorted. "Attention deficit is a requirement. So, have you been seeing this woman seriously?"

"I told you she was a client."

"*Was* a client. What is she now?"

"A friend. I think I mentioned that, too."

"Touchy." Ted looked at Selena's Web site. "I bet a creative woman like this could hold your interest."

"She could. She does."

"Tell me more."

"Not only is she creative, she's full of life. She has a smart mouth. And she's drop-dead gorgeous. To start."

"I can't believe it, Hermit Jack. This is a breakthrough."

"It would seem. For me."

"What does that mean?"

"Selena's very…self-reliant. She has a career. I'm not sure she's looking for a relationship. Besides, she has a twelve-year-old son. And you and I know all too well the pitfalls that lie between a boy and a man who isn't his father. A man interested in the mother."

"I shudder to remember." Ted's expression clouded. As much as their stepfather had tried to be fair, he had a difficult time liking Ted. Felt some drill-sergeant need to make a man of the younger, more gregarious, more creative brother. "But let's talk about brighter things. Ms. Milano. She sounds promising."

Although Selena might be the fire to melt Jack's ice, was she someone who could be *the* woman? She made it plain she wouldn't tolerate being dominated or even led. Is that how she saw commitment? He knew dominance and submission belonged in the animal world, not the human one, but Selena didn't seem to understand one could make that distinction. Why not?

"I don't know," he said.

"She agreed to skate with you on Friday."

"Sort of. I'd rolled it into a dog-handling package although I said I'd check with you about the dogs. Her son still wants to go if we have to leave them behind. That would mean Selena would go. But for me or Drew? Or both? I don't know. I can't really read her."

"A challenge." Ted's face lit up. "If there's anything that can get a Quinn's attention, it's a challenge."

"About the dogs." Jack wasn't used to so much talk centered on himself. "Can we bring them?"

"I wouldn't. Some people do, but it can

get very intense, depending on the crowd size. I wouldn't want to be a dog avoiding all those wheels and kneepads."

"Okay. I'll tell her. Them."

Ted pulled out his cell phone.

"Not now."

"If not now, when? Friday's in five days. A girl needs a little time to prepare. If for no reason but to put some glitter on her helmet. Dig out her Pippi Longstocking tights. You might not bring the dogs, but you need to bring some attitude."

Selena had plenty of attitude for both of them. *He* needed the time. Without the dogs, this was a date. As much as Selena had expressed reservations about that particular word, he had a few himself.

Ted thrust the phone inches from his nose. "I'm looking forward to meeting her. Any date of yours who has two legs as opposed to four is an improvement."

He took the phone and dialed the number Ted pointed to on the Web site. Maybe this time he'd get lucky with voice mail.

"Selena Milano." In person. But she didn't sound her usual spirited self.

"Is it a bad time? This is Jack."

"It's never quite a good time when you're lurking around, Quinn." Her voice wasn't playful, but caustic.

"What's going on?"

"Don't be coy. You must know I wouldn't be thrilled with you messing with Drew's head."

"You're going to have to fill me in, because I don't know what you're talking about."

"For twelve years, my son's been content with just him and me. Now, one afternoon with you, and he wants to find his father."

"Let's get one thing straight. Drew's been thinking about finding his father long before I came on the scene."

"Then why wouldn't he talk to me about it?"

"Because he didn't feel comfortable bringing it up. Didn't know how."

"And he felt comfortable with you because…?"

"I told him I didn't know my biological father."

"You see, that's what I don't get. A conversation like that doesn't seem very professional, seeing you were supposed to be teaching my son how to handle his dog. Not his life."

"He asked me outright if my father taught me my dog skills."

"And 'no' wasn't a sufficient enough answer?"

"It just came out." He didn't like being backed into a corner. "You can take some of the blame for that."

"I can, can I? How could you possibly turn this around on me?"

"Blame isn't the right word. But I took my cue from you. You treat Drew like a peer, not a kid. I can't see you lying to him if he asked you a direct question."

"I'm his mother. You're his dog handler. For three sessions. Which turned into four. One too many."

Ouch.

"I thought we'd gone beyond that stage, but it's clear I was wrong," he said, keeping his voice even. "Take care, Selena." He hung up only to face his brother.

"In the doghouse?" Ted speared a chunk of sticky rice with mango and offered it up. "Here. Have dessert before your main course. That always cheers me up."

"No thanks." He'd suddenly lost all appetite.

"Don't close down on me, Jack. Your conversation didn't sound good, but not good as in lovers' quarrel, which, in your case, is actually a very good thing. Well, if not quite good, then progress."

"We aren't lovers."

"Not yet. But there was heat in that dustup. Real potential. I think I saw a little hormonal steam come out of your ears. Hopefully, there's still fire in that furnace of yours."

"She doesn't want to see me again."

"Did she say those specific words?"

"Look, she's been a single mom the whole of her son's life. She has difficulty—legitimate difficulty, I'd say—sharing him. I offered him some advice, and she saw it as crossing a line."

"Was it good advice? Did the kid need to hear it?"

"Yes."

"I didn't hear you tell her that."

Jack glared at his brother, who could be persistent as untreated fleas.

"And you didn't answer my question," Ted continued. "Did she say the words, 'Jack Quinn, I never want to see you again'?"

"She didn't have to."

"I beg to differ. Unless she uttered those very words, she may actually be pushing you to see how much she and her son mean to you. How much you're willing to go through for them. Whether you're a quitter. And the Quinn boys aren't quitters. If we were, we'd have booked out long before Mom left Stepdaddy Dearest."

"Are you saying I should call Selena back?"

"No. Right now she's royally ticked, and the phone can be a horrible instrument of torture. No body language to help out. What you're going to do is go talk to her tomorrow." He turned toward the computer and the Web page still on the screen. "On the site of 'Swan Song.'"

How appropriate.

USUALLY Selena's work took her away to a place untroubled by everyday headaches like bills or adolescent angst or pesky boyfriends—not that What's His Name was a boyfriend—but today work was proving just another pain.

In the planning stages, "Swan Song" had

seemed like such a simple concept, a lark really. The block of buildings was destined to be demolished in six weeks, so she didn't have to worry about environmental impact. The property owners easily gave permission—the installation was good cultural buzz for the sparkling new complex they'd planned. The materials to make a two-octave wind harp that would attach to the frontage were laughably simple: two-by-fours that she could cut and attach at right angles to make *L*'s in sixteen incremental sizes, wire to string the harp, and assorted hardware. Selena was able to make a deal with Rupert, an old boyfriend and contractor she'd miraculously remained on good terms with. He'd let her scavenge his construction sites for remainders if she'd paint a foyer mural in a rehab he was doing on Russian Hill. In addition he'd help with assembling the harp. The electric company, the chief sponsor, would provide a cherry picker. The art interns would do whatever she asked. And San Francisco's ever-changing weather would play harpist for free.

But these best laid plans soon went awry.

The wooden frames they'd prefabbed and stored on site had been pilfered. Who the heck would want sixteen rough and unpainted *L*'s in various sizes? There'd been no time to re-canvass Rupert's sites, so an early trip to the lumber yard had started off this morning on a sour note. Selena hated using newly purchased materials when recycled ones had been so carefully culled. Then Rupert had hinted this barter agreement had merely been her way of saying she wanted to get back together. He'd leered at her ever since. Now, with the new frames finally in place along the frontage, the interns were bickering about the key they should tighten and tune the wires to as a steady drizzle made Selena's mop of curls tighten to the point where her reflection in the cherry picker truck's windshield showed not a cutting-edge artist, but a poodle in dire need of grooming. The only good thing about her definitely downgraded looks was Rupert had stopped leering.

"You can go," she said to him. "We'll finish up here."

She glanced at the driver of the electric company truck. Throughout the morning, he'd remained warm and dry with a thermos of coffee, a racing form and an iPod. Not once had he offered to help or shown the slightest interest in the project for which he was probably collecting overtime. Rain, complications in the project and the remnants of last night's conversation with Quinn made her uncharitable.

"I'll call you to set up a schedule for the mural," she reminded Rupert.

He gave a quick glance at her sodden state, a longer look at the unrelenting skies and headed for his truck. Although hunky, he'd never been more than a fair-weather friend to begin with. But why hadn't she noticed this flaw before? Was her taste in men changing?

The wind picked up, and the harp began a soft, eerie dirge. The interns cheered from the cherry picker bucket. Leave it to twenty-somethings to think a minor key cool. At the ripe old age of thirty-three she could have used something a bit more upbeat, but the sound did unquestionably alter the landscape, and that was the purpose of installation art.

"Makes you think the neighborhood is possessed."

She whirled around to face Quinn.

"And the beauty of it is," he continued, "a casual passerby will feel the hairs rise on the back of his neck, but unless he looks up, he won't know why."

It would be so much easier to dislike this guy if he didn't get her work. Easier, too, if he didn't look so doggone good. A little bit rumpled, but definitely at ease in the elements.

"What are you doing here?" she asked.

"I wanted to talk to you."

"How did you know where to find me?"

"Your Web site."

"I may have to rethink that. I make my schedule public to generate interest not encourage stalking."

He nodded at the interns being lowered in the cherry picker and the electric company driver. "You're chaperoned." He then pulled her under the building's overhang.

Once on the ground, the two students hopped from the bucket and, shaking like dogs fresh from a swim, ducked under the overhang as well. "It's working," the tall skinny one with the Vandyke said. "How awesome is that? Wanna go for a beer to celebrate? Between us, we think we can scrape enough change together to buy yours."

"I'll pass," she replied, mentally adding a sarcastic *Dude*. How immature did Vandyke sound? And was this the one she'd found marginally attractive? "I'm soaked through and freezing," she explained, "but I'll see you same time Wednesday in the library. We'll wind up the project by going over your portfolios and your grades."

"Later!" the students called, dashing in the direction of the nearest BART station. Or maybe the cheapest pub.

As soon as he'd secured the bucket, the electric company driver took off without as much as a wave.

And then there were two. So much for chaperones.

"I know you're angry with me for talking to Drew about his father," Quinn said without preamble, "but you can't keep him in a bubble. He's getting older. Forging his identity—"

"I don't need a lecture in human growth and development."

She thought about this morning before

she'd come to work. Drew had joined her in the kitchen for breakfast before he headed to school. There were none of the tears that had threatened last night. Only resolve. He'd stood by the sink and had said he wanted to go skating with her and Quinn on Friday whether the dogs could go or not. It sounded like fun. He'd said he didn't think what he wanted was unreasonable and he'd said it so calmly it almost hid the fact that he wanted something she didn't. That he felt the right to express that want. As an individual. Not an extension of his mother. No longer a child wholly under her control. The moment had shaken her.

She returned to the present to find Quinn looking at her. Waiting. His gaze penetrating.

"His...his father is not the easiest subject," she said at last. "For me."

"That's why I told him to talk to you before he did anything."

She laughed, but it came out more a hoarse bark. "To torture me?"

"No. To show respect for you."

The man didn't fight fair.

"I don't apologize for answering your

son's questions. The advice I gave him was sound."

"Do you get this involved with all your clients?" she asked.

"What do you think?"

"Then why such an interest in us?"

His look was disbelieving. "I thought it was obvious. I like Drew. I like you. A lot."

A simple answer. With so many possible complicated repercussions.

"If you want to run your thoughts by an adult," he said, "before sharing them with Drew, I'm a good listener. Besides, I've been on the other end of the stick. Drew's end. Your position's difficult, but ours isn't easy, either."

"I don't even want to run my thoughts by Drew. And I've known him for twelve years." Cold and wet and faced with this man who would not get out of her face—or her thoughts—she could feel her anger rising. "Do you realize what a hornets' nest you disturbed?"

"I said I'd be willing to have a discussion with you. I'm not willing to fight with you."

"Does anyone dare tell you to your face just how exasperating you are?"

"Look," he said, "I don't want to hang around where I'm not wanted. You decide the next step. I'm going skating this Friday night. No dogs. Just humans trying to connect with a good time. If you and Drew want to, meet me at Ferry Plaza at eight forty-five. If not, have a good life, Selena."

He walked away into the rain.

Suddenly cut adrift with the wind harp's sad plaint filling the air, Selena pulled out her cell phone and called Margo at the café.

"Sweetie, what's wrong?" Margo was mother to the world. The bistro had always been a safe port in a storm. How did that sitcom theme song go? A place where everybody knew your name. But at Margo's they didn't wear it out. Unlike chez Quinn.

"Do you have time to talk?"

"Absolutely," Margo replied. "It's the mid-afternoon lull. And Rosie's here. I'll hold her and we'll go in the back and draw the curtains. I'll have your espresso ready."

"Better make it a double."

When she stepped through the doorway to Margo's, the college student busing tables turned around, took one look at Selena and screamed. "I'm sorry!" the girl explained, laughing. "But you startled me!" She pointed to a mirror over the old-fashioned coatrack.

One glance told Selena why. From running her hands through her hair in absolute frustration, her poodle-do was now a spiky, slightly menacing disaster. Cujo had nothing on her. Moreover, mascara ran in black rivers down her cheeks. It looked as if the lunatic poodle needed a trip to the vet to take care of an eye infection as well as that comb-out. And maybe some doggie Valium thrown in for good measure. No wonder she'd run off all the men this afternoon. She reached in her pocket for a bandana to tame her curls and a tissue to wipe her face.

"What happened to you?" Margo asked, bustling over, helping her out of her sodden jacket.

"Occupational hazard."

"Let's get you into the annex and get a hot drink into you."

Selena felt better already. If someone could find a way to bottle Margo's essence, the world would be a safer, happier place. She let herself be nudged into the annex room that often got used in single-parent emergencies. Rosie uncurled from the over-stuffed sofa and rushed to hug her.

"Oh, Rosie! Long time, no see. How are you? And Hud and Casey?"

"I've never been better, and my men are wonderful. Casey just had his pediatric checkup, and his statistics are off the charts again. Hud's just getting his feet wet with this fatherhood shtick, and he's afraid Casey'll outstrip him before the year's out."

"I can't imagine Hud afraid of anything." Selena smiled at the image of the polished politician even the least bit unsettled by a five-year-old. "How's the campaign coming?"

"It's a whirlwind. I walked over from headquarters to hide out here for a bit and catch my breath."

As a single mom, Rosie had signed onto the Hudson McCloud mayoral campaign as a campaign manager and speech writer. Whirlwind might describe the campaign, but it also described Rosie's relationship with Hud. Although the election was yet to be decided, the two were now married.

"But for this afternoon, no politics." Rosie

drew her down onto the sofa. "Margo says you need boosting. What gives?"

As Margo placed a double espresso on the low table before her, Selena let her cares and worries spill. All of them. Quinn's interference. Drew's new alpha behavior. Her own insecurities. And, as always, the women listened.

Rosie took her hand. "I've learned something recently. The hard way. You can only control your own actions and reactions, not those of others."

"I'm not sure I want to hear that," Selena said, a painful knot forming along her shoulders. "My parents taught me to be in control. I always thought I was. Making a living. Creating a loving home. A stimulating environment for my son."

"There's a fine line between control…and dominance. And you know how you hate that word."

"Ouch! Am I domineering?"

The two other women looked at each other, until Rosie spoke. Cautiously. "We're your friends. But let's just say sometimes even we need a scorecard to know which

Selena's at bat. The carefree artist…or the woman who wants things her way or the highway."

"You're not suggesting Drew knows what's best for him, are you? He's only twelve."

"In some cultures, he's a man," Margo remarked, her words gentle. "He has to learn to make his own decisions, no matter how difficult. Sooner or later, he's going to move beyond your control. It seems to me it would be easier to untie the apron strings gradually rather than have them unceremoniously lopped off. Of course, my Ellie's only eleven and Peter's only seven, so you have to promise to give me this pep talk over the next few years. Repeatedly, perhaps."

Selena sighed. "I…I feel like a…failure somehow."

"Nonsense!" Rosie declared. "You're a wonderful mother and we're not going to let anyone—even you—run yourself down. You're entering a new phase of life, that's all."

"That's all! You make it sound so simple."

"Everyone in our circle knows exactly how difficult the role of single parent is,"

Margo assured her. "How difficult transitions are. We're here to give you support. For the next step."

"I'm not sure what the next step is." The admission was one Selena hadn't dared make before. Not even to herself. "I've wrapped myself up in Drew, but I've been blind to the fact he'd want to know about his father no matter how much I threw myself into both roles. I shouldn't be so upset. He's just asking for information. He even said he doesn't know what he wants to do with it."

Rosie seemed hesitant. "Selena...Drew isn't the only one who needs to think long and hard about the next step."

"What do you mean?"

"You need to think about the future, too. About what your life will be like as Drew grows up. Ask yourself this. In six, maybe ten years, when he's graduated high school, college, what do you see yourself doing? And will you be doing it alone?"

"We're not talking about Drew's father anymore, are we?"

"Personally," Margo said, "I'm wondering why you're resisting the chance at a real adult relationship. Why you're resisting Jack Quinn. Compared to the other guys you date, he sounds so substantial. What would it hurt to accept a little offered help from him? Talk to him about his experience as a boy. About Drew's present conflict. He's showing a real interest. Drew likes him. And he's been in Drew's shoes."

"Beyond that," Rosie added, "what would it hurt if you went skating Friday night? It's a group thing, right? You can get to know Jack better without that dating pressure. Have some fun with him and your son. You might find yourself open to new possibilities. And if it doesn't work out? You've never before had difficulty breaking off with a guy. Come on, Selena. Let go a little."

She felt ambushed. By these two women who had found love again. Who were so flush with newlywed bliss they wanted to see the world paired off.

But Rosie had made some valid points. Selena had never thought of the future other than in terms of her and Drew. A family unit. In the now. She'd ignored the probability that Drew would move away, or at the very least out of their loft. Leaving her alone. Really alone.

It hurt that Rosie had questioned her openness to new possibilities. As an artist, Selena had always considered herself Ms. Possibility Personified. But was she being honest with herself? At least where relationships were concerned? How open was she if she couldn't even handle a night of skating?

Rosie's last comment concerned her most, however. The one about breaking off with Quinn if it didn't work out. You see, Quinn was different. As she'd witnessed at her loft, he was a soup-to-nuts-and-stay-for-the-after-dinner-show kind of guy whereas she was a sample-the-smorgasbord-and-run kind of gal. At least she had been until he'd come along. The damnedest thing was he had her wondering now what it might be like not to break it off before the dessert cart and the after-dinner drinks appeared.

What it might be like to actually stick around for ham and eggs the next morning.

And that thought really rattled her.

CHAPTER EIGHT

"SHE'S NOT COMING." Jack stood at the entrance to Ferry Plaza and scanned the crowd.

"Oh, ye of little faith," Ted replied as he skated in circles to the disco beat that blared from a portable sound system. Traditionally, the Midnight Rollers boogied as they assembled until their founder and master of ceremonies gave the signal at the dot of nine to begin the city roll.

Jack wasn't up for the fun and games. Not without Selena and Drew. His skates and helmet remained on a bench.

"Does she have a friend or relative with green hair?"

Jack's head jerked in the direction Ted pointed to see Selena approaching with Drew and Maxine. If a crowd and a bodyguard was what it took to get Selena to meet up with him, the more the merrier.

"Maxine," Ted said after the introductions. Jack had warned him not to rush at Selena should she come. So his brother made himself busy applying reflective tape from a roll he carried to everyone's helmets, skates and jackets. "Have you ever skated before?"

"Young man, don't patronize me. I've been on wheels since my skates were heavy metal side-by-sides and I had to strap them on my shoes." Right now Maxine was putting on state-of-the-art in-lines and a helmet that looked as if it came out of a sci-fi adventure. "It's Selena who's never tried it."

Jack stared at Selena in surprise.

"How hard can it be?" she said with a shrug. "I borrowed skates and a helmet from one of my neighbors who's a self-professed klutz."

"If it's your first time out," he replied, "you might wish we'd brought the dogs. To tow you back from Fisherman's Wharf."

"Drew said the same thing on the way over. Have you two never heard of cabs?"

"Speaking of cabs," Ted interjected, "I

hope you're thinking of hitching a ride *inside* one. There's a hard and fast rule about obeying all traffic rules, lights and signs and not hanging on the outside of vehicles. Some people thought that was the easy way to make the hills, but the Midnight Rollers reached a truce with the city by showing we're law abiding citizens. Although we're almost an institution now—a tourist attraction, in fact—and city drivers and the police know to look out for us, be careful out there."

Jack was glad to see his brother performing the role of skate ambassador rather than the matchmaker he'd too often acted in the past.

"Don't worry." Selena patted a fanny pack. "I brought money. For food, drink and emergency phone calls."

"In that case, let me make a suggestion," Ted added. "It's not a rule, but it's wise to buddy up. Catch up with the rest of the group at agreed upon stops along the way. So, Drew, can you skate as well as Maxine?"

"You bet. She's the one who taught me."

"Then you two are a natural buddy team." His brother sounded so innocent. So suspiciously innocent. "That leaves Selena with

Jack, and, if this is Selena's first time on skates, the two of you should maybe stick to sidewalks wherever possible. I'll run interference between my regular group and your two. Of course, we'll part ways at Fisherman's Wharf because I'll be doing the rest of the route. Hurry. Get those skates on. We're about to receive our send-off." He began to skate circles around them as the disco beat increased in volume and intensity.

"Drew!" Selena shouted over the music. She sat on a bench and struggled with her skates. "I think we should all stick together."

"Mom!" Drew and Maxine were already up and following Ted's moves. "I came to skate, not poke around!"

"He'll be fine with me," Maxine assured her. She sounded almost as innocent as Ted. "That is if you don't mind buddying with Selena, Jack."

"Buddies," Selena muttered. "How ridiculous."

"I don't mind," he told Maxine and knelt to help Selena with her skates. "Stop halfway up the Embarcadero, and we'll catch up with you there."

Selena shot him an eyes-narrowed glance.

"Too optimistic?" he asked as he lifted the borrowed helmet and adjusted it on her head.

She tried to wrest the straps away from him, but managed only in getting her fingers tangled up in his. "As I said before, how hard can this be?"

The music ended, and with great fanfare the master of ceremonies declared the run begun. Maxine, Drew and Ted took off, tendrils of fog swirling round them. It was the kind of light fog that crept and wound and intermittently showed a few stars in a twinkling effect that competed with the glitter and bling and iridescent Lycra on many of the skaters. Jack stood and offered Selena his hand. She ignored it. But no sooner had she pushed herself upright than she was flat on her backside on the ground.

"Don't say it," she snapped, rolling to her knees.

They might be at this bench for the duration, but he'd be the last to say I told you so. And the very last to complain about being left behind as a twosome.

"Let me help you get your bearings." He bent down and, encircling her waist, lifted her to a standing position. Then held her close so that she wouldn't fall again. Or that's what he told himself.

She couldn't seem to keep her feet under her. "Don't they make these things with training wheels?"

He held her tighter.

"I sense you're enjoying this, Quinn."

"That you decided to come tonight? Yes, I'm glad." He wasn't about to equivocate.

"I meant my flailing around in what could be interpreted as helplessness."

"Pity the fool who chooses that interpretation."

"Be serious." She pushed away from him, but held tightly to his upper arms.

"Serious? Okay. Am I gloating over the fact that you can't skate? No. Do I like you hanging all over me? Absolutely."

"Me? Hanging all over you? In your dreams." As if to prove her point, she let go of him and stood very, very still, biting her lower lip. She looked so intent, so adorable. Like an angry imp.

"Now that you can stand," he said, "let's try this. I'll push from behind."

"And why would you do that?"

"Aside from the fact I like touching you, it'll give you your sea legs, so to speak. When you feel sure enough to strike out on your own, go for it."

"Does it embarrass you to be stuck with an unskilled skater?" she asked. The Midnight Rollers were long gone. Nobody left to see just the two of them.

"No. Does it embarrass you to accept help?"

"Um…"

"Can't say it, can you? All right. Looks like I'll have to take over as pack leader." Before she could protest, he skated behind her, grasped her waist, then gently propelled her forward.

She squeaked, and he felt her whole body tense.

"Are your eyes open?"

When she nodded her head, he picked up speed. "Relax. Unlock your knees. Forget you're on skates."

"Easy for you to say. You're not the one out front, catching bugs in your teeth."

"That's why they make toothpicks. Stop complaining and talk to me. It'll relax you."

"Talk? A-about what?"

"Tell me about your first installation."

"My very first?" She squeaked again in protest as he maneuvered her over a series of cracks in the sidewalk. "That…that would be my senior prom." She managed a tentative chuckle, and he felt her relax a little. "I was in charge of decorations. The theme was 'Black & White.' I think the administration envisioned a high school version of the city's black-and-white ball or maybe old Fred and Ginger movies."

"But?" He couldn't see her following any suggestions, let alone those.

She began to shift her weight from side to side in a beginning stroking movement. She had a lithe athletic build, and he had no doubt she'd quickly get the hang of skating.

"But I hung the walls of the Hyatt with sheets dyed black, then looped toilet paper from the ceiling. Administration was furious, but Maxine was proud of me and most of the kids thought it was cool. I guess you could say that's when I was bitten by the installation bug."

Midway through her story he'd taken his

hands from her waist, leaving her skating on her own. She wasn't ready for roller derby, but she was fairly steady on her feet. Now he moved alongside her. Took her hand. Felt a hint of thaw come over the emotions he'd put on ice these past five years.

Even stepping back into the dating world had left him cold. All the superficial rituals of the chase. Boring. Pointless. His marriage, which had ended far too soon, had been a good one. He missed the intimacy of a lasting relationship. But in dating how did you begin to be honest about wanting to cut to the substance without looking like some needy nutcase? He hadn't figured that dilemma out. Until now he hadn't found a woman who interested him enough to try.

Until Selena.

"You tricked me," she said softly.

Actually, she didn't mind. She was still stunned she was skating. Thanks to Quinn, a man of surprising and alluring talents, the foremost of which was the ability to let someone lean on him for as long as needed without making that someone feel small. Reason enough not to remove her hand from his. Then there was how good it felt. She hadn't held hands with a guy since grade school. Holding hands wasn't something a hip SWF did these days. Hop in bed, yes. Kiss, maybe. Hold hands, too intimate.

It was sort of like using his first name rather than his last.

A Midnight Roller barreled out of the mist toward them. Jack's brother. Somewhere he'd acquired two long purple feathers that protruded from the back of his helmet. "Hey, kids, just checking on you." Ted glanced at their joined hands, then grinned like the Cheshire Cat. "But I see things are good. Very good."

"What about the others?" Jack asked before she could.

"Drew and Maxine are a short distance up ahead. Near Pier 23. They'll wait till you catch up. It's not far."

"Are they resting?" she asked, a little worried about her son. This was a workout.

"Resting? No way. They're dancing with the rest of the Rollers entertaining the tourists. I think Drew's drinking martinis." In a flash Ted was gone. "Just kidding," came his disembodied voice from out of the fog.

"You two are brothers?" she asked, slightly amazed.

"Yeah. But he's the introvert."

Maneuvering around a manhole cover, she squeezed Quinn's hand and surprised herself by appreciating his steady strength. "You've managed to get me to tell you all about myself," she said. "My family, my art, even my high school prom, but you haven't said much about yourself beyond the work you do with dogs."

"What you see is what you get."

She sensed he was uncomfortable with the prospect of talking about himself.

"What were you like growing up? What was your family like? Now's the time to speak, Fido."

"There's not much to say beyond my work. My past is ancient history. I like to stay in the present."

"I'm not letting you off that easily. Here I am, skating the streets of San Francisco after dark with a guy I know very little about. For the moment, it's just the two of us and me without my mace. I don't want to end up a damsel in distress. Or a headline in the

Chronicle. Enlighten me. Give me a heads-up. Or at least a head start."

She meant her words to be banter, a bit of sass, nothing more, but he stopped skating and pulled her to stand in front of him, looked her directly in the eye.

"You know everything you need to know about me if you'd admit it," he said, his words even and contained, but his eyes full of intensity. "And I want to hear what you know."

This was not a guy like others in her life.

"Are you always so straightforward?"

The muscles along his jaw relaxed. "Straightforward. That's one."

"You really want to play this game?"

"I don't want to play games with you, Selena."

For the first time in her life, she didn't want to engage in that old feint and parry, either.

"You're good with animals," she said. "And kids. And your brother seems to love you."

She thought she saw him wince.

"You're very self-contained." An attribute

she found a little daunting, until it suddenly hit her that self-contained wasn't too far removed from self-reliant. Her own personal fave. The difference was only a matter of style and of who was on the controlling end.

"Isn't all that enough to know about someone?" he asked. "For starters."

She'd slept with men about whom she'd known less.

"This is what I know about you," he continued, with a look that pierced her. "You're a great parent. A super creative artist. Funny. Stubborn. Sexy. A terrific cook. A messy housekeeper. And, oh, yeah, kissing makes you hiccup."

"It does not!"

"You're one for one as far as I'm concerned."

"What a cheesy, backhanded way to sample another." She laughed in spite of herself. "I take back that you're straightforward."

"I wasn't fishing, believe me. I was being observant. Now if I'd wanted a kiss, I'd have said, 'Kiss me.'"

"Were you just saying what you would have said or were you actually saying it? For real."

"Let's make it clear then." He pulled her close. "Kiss me."

"What if this is where my stubborn rather than my sexy side shows up?"

"Hut!"

Had he just given her the dog command? Before she could protest, his mouth moved over hers.

The man could flat-out kiss.

With the night air cool and damp, she might have settled for some extremely warm interaction, but while her brain and lips thought one thing, her feet-on-wheels thought something else altogether. Without warning, she found herself dangerously close to chipping a front tooth on his belt buckle.

Once again he saved her from falling for him totally.

"I never thought of myself as a guy who knocked women off their feet."

"Don't flatter yourself." Actually, there was no reason why he shouldn't.

He took her hand, a lovely look of seduction in his eyes, but he surprised her by saying, "Come on. Let's find the others."

"You don't want to finish what you started?"

"There'll be plenty of other times."

"Are you always this damned sure of yourself?"

"I'm sorry," he said, the corners of his rather yummy mouth twitching. "Did you want to continue kissing? You only have to say so. Or make the next move."

"Oh, ho! I'm to come to you? And if I do, it'll then be, 'Sit, Selena. Guard the door, Selena. Fetch my pipe and slippers, Selena.'"

He laughed, and she wasn't sure if he hadn't laughed in her presence before or if she'd just now noticed how sensuous it was. He was. "I don't smoke," he said. "And the point is this isn't going to work if you don't do exactly what *you* want to do. But, come on, Selena. It's a dog-eat-dog world out there. There's safety—and fun and excitement—in numbers. Let someone else into your personal pack."

He laced his fingers with hers and pulled her toward Pier 23, leaving her to concentrate on her footwork at the same time to wonder what exactly it was she wanted. This time. With Quinn an intriguing and formidable presence on her horizon.

"Are we there yet?" she asked with mock petulance.

"Not quite, but we've made a good start."

Somehow she didn't think he was talking about skating.

As they continued in silence, Selena found the need to adjust her dating mindset. Quinn's ease with the lull in conversation brought other guys to mind. Take Rupert, the fair-weather contractor. Please. They'd dated on and off for three months, but even after twelve weeks Rupert still felt the need to impress her. With too much boastful talk. Too much strutting. Too much Rupert in her face altogether. She couldn't picture him skating behind the crowd. Too many missed opportunities to show off.

But Quinn? Wherever he went, whatever the situation he was in, he was an enormous presence without the posturing. Engaged, yet somehow aloof. With a hint of mystery, no matter that he claimed what you saw was what you got.

Reggae music drifted through the fog before the outlines of the old restaurant on Pier 23 appeared like faint lines on a much-used Etch A Sketch.

"Tired?" Quinn asked.

"No. Surprisingly, I'm getting the hang of this. But my hands are cold. Do you think there's coffee somewhere?"

Just as she asked, the fog lifted, showing the parking lot where skaters and restaurant patrons mingled happily, some of the diners snapping pictures of the skaters. One couple, skating and juggling and dressed in matching bumblebee costumes, drew particular attention. At the entrance to the lot a half-dozen push-carts had set up business, selling drinks and food. Maxine and Ted stood chatting next to one, their hands cupped around steaming drinks. A short distance away— Selena couldn't believe her eyes—Drew was engaged in a rather flirtatious conversation with a cute girl his age. Would wonders never cease? Whenever they got together with Derrick and Bailey, twelve-year-old Leslie totally intimidated her son. Perhaps it was the fog or the adult feel of after-hours on the streets, but there was a little magic afoot tonight. Selena herself had felt it. In Quinn's embrace. In his decided interest but his refusal to give all of himself to her all at once.

"Coffee or hot chocolate?" he asked.

"Ooh, hot chocolate sounds good. Thanks. I'll be over there with Maxine and Ted."

"Are you sure?" He glanced at her feet. "I'll just be a minute if you want to wait for me."

"Now you're underestimating me."

"Never."

He seemed so sincere he caught her off guard. This was not a guy whose emotions you'd toy with. She needed to think things through before she took their relationship a step beyond a couple of enticing kisses. Beyond tonight.

As he headed to get their drinks, she coasted toward Maxine and Ted, who seemed to cut their conversation short as she approached. Were these two already plotting something? Maxine gave Selena's upright stance a look of approval, then moved away. "I think I see an old flame," she explained over her shoulder before disappearing into the crowd.

"So, how are the feet?" Ted asked. "No blisters I hope."

"No. Not yet." She patted her fanny pack. "Don't tell anyone—especially not your brother—but I did bring Band-Aids. Just in case."

"Don't tell me you're another one who hides their pain."

"Another one?"

"My big brother. An alligator could be gnawing on his leg, but would he call for help? No. He'd just bop the creature on the head, then crawl back to his pack of dogs and whittle himself a peg leg while the stump healed. Iron Jack."

"Harsh."

"I don't mean it to be. Now if you or I had a leg down a gator's gullet, Jack would risk his life to save ours. His greatest strength is also his greatest weakness. He takes saving the world very seriously. Me, when we were kids. His wife. His dogs—"

"His wife?"

Ted's look was sympathetic. "Of course he wouldn't tell you about Anneka. I think he feels guilty he couldn't save her. But disease and death can have a single-mindedness of their own. We're only human. We're not really in control."

She didn't agree with the control assessment, but now didn't seem the time to argue. "Your brother hasn't told me much about himself."

"And he wouldn't like me telling you. But I thought you needed to know that he's incredibly courageous and loyal. And he needs someone who can match his strength. Someone he can lean on occasionally. Who knows? Maybe someone else who hides the Band-Aids."

Warning bells went off. All this talk of leaning on one another? Possible commitment ahead? Flashing lights. Exercise caution. Maybe a thanks and an evasive, "See ya," were called for at the end of this evening. She needed to get her head around Ted's revelation, both content and purpose.

Before she could, however, Quinn skated up, cups of hot chocolate in hand, Drew alongside.

"Hey, Mom!" Drew exclaimed. "Jack said he'd come to my school next week during the career fair. Said he'd talk about dog handling while Axel and I demonstrate. Cool, huh?"

So not cool.

In the first place, she'd always been

Drew's guest speaker during career awareness week. Second, she hadn't even decided if she was up to the seriousness of seeing Quinn again. She'd suspected and Ted had all but confirmed that Quinn wasn't casual fling material. She wasn't sure she was anything more. Thirdly, she wasn't used to her son making his own decisions.

Her girlfriends had talked about her taking the "next step" in her life. About letting go. It was one thing to decide what that step was and to take it willingly. It was another thing to be blindfolded and pushed down the escalator.

CHAPTER NINE

SOMETHING HAD CHANGED. Jack could feel it. In the time it took to get two cups of hot chocolate, Selena had distanced herself from him.

She'd been talking with Ted, and that could mean anything. But his brother had melted into the crowd. Now she stared at Drew as if she wanted to say something, but couldn't find the words. Jack didn't understand. After their talk about Drew and adolescents and self-esteem, he thought she'd be ecstatic her son wanted to get up in front of a group of kids, his peers. Wanted to show off his newfound skills.

Instead, she looked troubled and focused on something she wasn't sharing.

New at skating, she should have focused on keeping her feet under her. Another skater brushed perilously close. As Selena moved to keep from getting her hot chocolate bumped, she lost her balance and went down, throwing her free hand behind her to break her fall. Upon impact a look of pain crossed her face, and she came up cradling her left wrist. Both Drew and Jack knelt beside her at the same time, but Drew looked to Jack to take the lead.

He gently cupped her arm, then felt her wrist. "I've examined enough broken dog bones to think you have a nasty sprain here. But I'm no doctor. We need to get you to the emergency room for X-rays."

"No!" Selena's swift response was emphatic. "Drew and I'll take a cab home. Maxine can drive the Honda back when she's done skating. No need to spoil everyone's evening. I'll be fine after some rest."

Drew's look of resignation indicated he might have witnessed his mother's super-woman act on more than one occasion.

Maxine and Ted skated up, and Jack looked to Maxine for support. "Can you convince her to get this wrist checked?"

Selena glared at her friend.

Maxine seemed to understand the warning. "Selena knows her own body. If the wrist doesn't improve, she'll seek help."

"Band-Aid anyone?" Ted asked caustically as he shot a pointed glance at Selena.

Selena tried to take her skates off, but it was clearly a two-handed task.

"Drew," Jack said, "you get one. I'll get the other. Maxine, get Selena's car keys out of her fanny pack. Ted, get us a cab."

"Us?" Selena asked, her tone frosty.

"If you're not going to the hospital, I'm not leaving you alone."

"I have Drew."

Drew looked at his mother down on the ground, her face showing obvious pain. "I'd feel better if Jack came, too."

"What about your truck?" The ice in her words made it obvious she wasn't about to soften her protest. Cede her control.

"Ted drove. Up you go." He lifted her to her feet, felt her sway a little. "Dizzy?"

"No." He could tell she wasn't about to admit it, but she leaned on Drew as they walked to the curb to wait for the taxi. "Maxine," she said, "promise me you won't cut your skating short. Bring the Honda back whenever."

Maxine looked at Selena as if she was used to giving the younger woman space but, at times like this, didn't like it. "Don't worry about my skating." Although her words might be gruff, her voice sounded concerned.

Drew helped his mother into the cab when it came, then made room for Jack. When Selena wouldn't look at him, Jack wondered again what, beyond her injured wrist, was bugging her. One of the things he liked about working with dogs was that they lived in the moment. No matter the traumas they might have suffered, dogs could be brought to live happily in the present. Humans, however, accumulated and dragged around a life's worth of emotional baggage. How heavy was Selena's load? What was keeping her from meeting him halfway?

At the downstairs entrance to her apartment, she fumbled with her good hand for cab fare even as Jack handed the driver a bill and told him to keep the change. Glowering, she refused both Jack's and Drew's help to the sidewalk, then took her first tottering step.

Knowing severe pain could make the strongest individual unsteady, Jack scooped her into his arms before she knew what hit her. "Drew, get the doors. And, whatever you do, don't let Axel jump."

He had a Rottweiler at his center who weighed more than Selena, but even the Rottie was easier to carry than this woman weighed down by sputtering, wordless indignation.

Drew took the lead, clearing the path ahead, unlocking the door, making Axel sit to the side once they were in the loft.

"Which way's your room?" he asked Selena.

She tried to push away, to put her feet on the floor. "One more step and I'll consider this a home invasion."

"You'll get over it," he replied, tightening his hold on her, following Drew.

Her room was just like her. Eye-popping. A riot of colors and textures and contradictions. He carefully made his way over a floor strewn with clothing to what might or might not be a bed. Only when he stubbed his toe on a castor and spotted pillows did he lower her and let her go. Of course, she tried to get up.

"Sorry," he said. "You're not going anywhere until Drew gets you an anti-inflammatory and a glass of water. I saw an all-night drugstore down the block. I'll take Axel on a relief run, and bring back a flexible bandage to bind up your wrist."

"Quinn, I'm adding *pushy* to that list we started for you," she said, but, lying on the bed, she seemed to have lost some of her fight. "I can get my own Advil."

"Listen to Jack, Mom." Drew headed for the bathroom. "Let us take care of you." There was an authority to the boy's tone that appeared to surprise his mother. Unsettle her, even. But that could just be pain.

Leaving Selena in Drew's hands, Jack found Axel's leash by the door, then headed for the drugstore with the dog. When they returned, Selena had changed into an over-sized T-shirt and had gotten under the covers of her bed. The anti-inflammatory must have already begun to bring some relief because the pain lines between her eyebrows had eased. He wished he could say the same for the fiery displeasure that still flashed in her eyes.

"Jack, do you want something to eat?" Drew called from the kitchen.

"He's leaving," Selena snapped back.

"Not until I bandage your wrist," he insisted, sitting on the edge of the bed. While the rest of the apartment smelled of her art supplies, her room smelled gently floral and very feminine. "And while I'm at it, do you want to tell me why you're so angry with me all of a sudden?"

She hesitated. "I'm angry with myself for getting hurt." She avoided eye contact as if this was a half truth. "The State University project is ready for installation. I'm not much good with a bum arm."

He carefully wound the elasticized bandage around her wrist, which already showed signs of swelling. Her arm was tense with reluctance to let him do the job. "You can still be the brains. Let Maxine and the interns do the physical stuff."

"That's not how I work."

He wasn't going to argue the point with her. He was feeling a need to pick his battles. "So you're not angry with me?"

She still didn't meet his eye. "I'm not… *angry* with you."

"Are you going to make me guess the adjective that best describes how you're feeling?" Having fastened the end of the bandage, he turned her face so that she had to look at him. "That could take all night."

"I'm…not used to people telling me what to do."

"Men, in particular."

"Mom," Drew said, entering the room, "you should get some sleep."

"Even my kid thinks he knows what's best for me," she said in a huff, pulling the covers over her head. "Now get lost. Both of you."

It hit Jack then that she was having trouble with Drew's emerging confidence. With the prospect of him becoming a man. With the thought of losing control of her little boy. Of losing a life as she'd known it for twelve years. All that couldn't be easy. Especially not for a woman like Selena.

He rose to follow Drew from the room.

"I made grilled cheese sandwiches," Drew said quietly. "I made you a couple, too."

"Thanks. I didn't realize how hungry I was."

In the kitchen, the sandwiches were already on plates and juice poured in two glasses, two stools pulled up to the big central butcher's block. For some reason the boy's simple consideration—the inclusion—moved Jack. Maybe Selena wasn't the only one who resisted being taken care of. He hadn't known how good relief could feel until it was thrust upon him.

Drew suddenly looked worried. "Is my mom going to be okay?"

"I think so, sure. Tonight will tell. If she can't sleep from pain. If she runs a fever. Those are things you'll have to watch for. If she gets worse in any way, you'll have to call a cab for the emergency room. Even if she protests." What was he saying? The poor kid looked exhausted. There was no way he could stay up all night, keeping watch. Besides he was only twelve. "Would you feel better if I slept on the sofa?"

"Yeah." Relief showed in every inch of the preteen's slight body.

And for the first time in a long time, Jack felt good because someone—someone without four paws and a tail—needed him.

SELENA AWOKE to a throbbing in her wrist and the sound of low voices from her kitchen. Drew, Maxine…and Quinn. For a person who wanted nothing better than to crawl back under her covers to think and heal away from prying eyes, the day was not starting off well.

Careful of the bandaged wrist—Quinn's controlling ministrations of the previous night came sharply to mind—she made her way to the bathroom, popped a couple more Advil and brushed her teeth clumsily. Being left-handed with an out-of-commission south paw wasn't going to be a walk in the park. But, hey, ever since Quinn's arrival in her life, a simple walk in the park wasn't a walk in the park, either. She had half a mind to go back to bed without a "good morning" to the others, but the aroma of coffee, toast and eggs drew her and her very empty stomach into the kitchen…where her son, her good friend and mentor and the thorn in her side sat, eating, chatting and sharing the morning paper as if they were family.

"How are you feeling?" Maxine asked, getting another mug and pouring coffee.

"What are you doing here?" Selena asked Jack. Surely injury could be counted a fair excuse for rudeness.

"I slept on the sofa."

"My sofa?"

"It's my sofa, too, Mom," Drew said, "and I asked Jack to stay."

"A wise decision, boys," Maxine said, very deliberately placing the mug of coffee in Selena's good hand, then giving her a warning look. "It might have turned out you needed something. Like the emergency room after all."

"I'm fine."

"We saved you some eggs," Drew said, giving her his stool at the butcher's block. "Jack made 'em."

"You people are hovering."

"So sue us." Quinn reached across the butcher block. "Let me see that wrist."

She held back. "You said yourself you weren't a doctor."

"Give him your arm, Mom." Drew held the plate of eggs and toast above her head. "Or no breakfast." To Quinn he said, "Don't mind her. She's always grouchy before she has her coffee."

"Then let's set up an IV. A caffeine drip. Stat." While she reached for the plate with her right hand, Quinn took her left arm and began to unwind the bandage.

Her stomach rumbled. Okay, so she'd let him look to his heart's content. She'd pretend that arm wasn't even attached to her body. But trying to feed herself with her unaccustomed right hand made her feel like a toddler. After she made a couple unsuccessful stabs with the fork, Maxine pushed a spoon in her direction. The humiliation.

"My guess is your wrist is badly bruised, but not broken," Quinn said, rebandaging her arm. "If I were you, I'd still have it checked by a doctor."

"That's not what your brother said you'd do." She was satisfied at the look of surprise in his eyes. "Besides, you're not me."

"Could someone get this woman more coffee?" Quinn rose. "Ready to shove off, Drew?"

"Wait a minute! Where are you going? This is Saturday. Drew always walks me to Margo's Bistro on Saturdays."

"Not today, Mom. Jack and I are going to his center to work up a demonstration for school. Career week, remember?"

"Did you ask permission?"

"Cool your jets," Maxine admonished. "He asked me. We didn't know how long you'd sleep, so I gave my permission."

They had teamed up against her. All of them. And were determined to undermine her hold on her world. *Her* world. Didn't they know possessive pronouns had been created for a reason?

Drew seemed to sense her hurt. "Mom, is it okay? If you want me to walk with you, I will."

She was being an absolute jerk. A silly, self-centered whiner. So, knowing it, why was it hard to stop? "You go," she finally managed to say. "Even with a bandaged wrist I think I can make it to Margo's alone." She pinned Maxine with a squinty-eyed stare. "You're not planning on babysitting me, are you?"

"I wouldn't think of it. I just brought your car back. Besides, I have a date."

"You do?"

"Someone Ted introduced me to last night. A retired businessman. A fantastic skater with a great sense of humor. We're going to the farmers' market. He's an expert on organic honey. In fact he's thinking of coming out of retirement to start a little apiary up in Sonoma. Funny how a man with a bee in his bonnet sounds sexy."

"But a businessman? Maxine, I'm surprised. That is so not your type!"

"Don't listen to her." Quinn glanced Maxine's way as he and Drew headed out with Axel. "I like a woman who can step outside her comfort zone."

"Ooh, zinger!" Maxine rolled her eyes toward Selena. "Did I mention I love a man with a *challenging* sense of humor?"

"Oh, this one's as funny as a crutch," Selena grumbled.

Over his shoulder Jack said, "I'll have Drew home midafternoon."

And that was that.

"Badly done, Selena. Badly done," Maxine scolded in a paraphrased line from one of Selena's favorite Jane Austen novels. "Jack deserves better."

"I didn't ask him to step beyond his role as dog handler."

"That he dared venture past your prickly, off-putting behavior is testament to his strength of character. Besides, what are you afraid of?"

"I'm not afraid of anything." She toyed with her uneaten eggs. "But he seems to want more than I'm willing to give."

"What exactly would you sacrifice if you entered a relationship with him?"

"I don't know. That's why it seems wiser to stick to plan. Things are a lot less complicated with just Drew and me. And an occasional, very casual boyfriend."

Maxine gently took both Selena's hands in hers. "Tell me again where you got this etched-in-stone plan."

"You know how I was raised. To be independent. Self-reliant. Berta and Rocco instilled those traits in me. Now they're second nature. And you know about old habits dying hard."

"I don't know anything about old habits, but I do know it's time you faced up to the curse of Berta and Rocco."

"The curse?"

"Maybe that's going too far. But at the very least, hypocrisy."

"Maxine! What are you talking about?"

"Berta and Rocco might have preached independence and self-reliance, but they did it from a couple's pulpit. They've lived their lives as a twosome, joined at the hip, supporting each other." Maxine kissed Selena on the forehead. A rare show of affection. "Open your eyes. Practice a little of what your parents *did*, not so much what they *said*."

Selena found herself speechless.

"Also, that self-reliant plan of yours, that independence your parents raised you to…maybe you think if you give it up, if you find happiness in a shared life, it lays bare Berta and Rocco's excuse for leaving you. Maybe you'd have to get righteously—and rightfully—pissed at them for booking out early on you and Drew. What if they didn't consciously try to make you self-reliant? What if they were just selfish and followed their own little collective dream?"

Dumbfounded, Selena tried unsuccessfully to recall a time when her mentor had ever before criticized her parents.

Maxine gathered up her keys. "Enjoy your time at Margo's. At least with that crew I know you won't be alone."

Well, gee, if she hadn't before, she sure felt alone now—alone and thoroughly misunderstood—as she showered with her bandaged left arm outside the shower curtain and made a mess of the bathroom, as she fumbled to dress and ended up in worn sweats and a pair of old work clogs, as she trudged to the café with fittingly dark clouds hanging overhead.

A small, niggling part of her had always wondered if her parents had raised her to take care of herself, or if, tired of taking care of her, they'd just moved on. Berta and Rocco had a history of loving humanity. Individuals gave them headaches.

Inside Margo's Bistro, Selena lifted her hand in a half-hearted wave to Derrick and Robert, who were chatting at the counter, but headed straight for the annex where Margo, Nora, Bailey and Rosie were laughing so hard Bailey was doubled over, clutching her stomach.

"What's so funny?" Selena could use a good laugh about now.

Glancing at each other, the women sobered.

"Oh, we were just talking about… husbands," Nora said.

Margo started to get up. "I'll get your espresso."

"Please, don't wait on me. You look so

comfortable, and I've had people hovering over me all morning. I'll get something to drink later." Selena slumped into a chair. "And it's okay, guys. Just because I don't have one, doesn't mean you can't talk about husbands."

"Did you go skating?" Margo asked.

"I don't want to talk about it."

"What happened to your wrist?"

"I don't want to talk about that, either."

"Well, Rosie's downloaded something she thinks we'll all want to talk about."

Rosie, speechwriter and former member of the high-school debate team, was fascinated with data. Statistics. Factual information. Studies. She was always bringing pertinent downloads to their meetings for discussion. Until now the discussions had mostly revolved around children and childrearing. Single parenthood. Now she shuffled photos—head shots of men?—as if she were about to deal a hand of cards.

"Rosie," Margo said, "the floor's all yours."

"This study comes out of the University of California at Santa Barbara." Rosie indicated a sheaf of papers on the coffee table. "I downloaded the whole thing if anyone's

interested. But the upshot is this. Women—
if we're honest—are supposed to be able to
look at a man's face alone and tell if he's
father or fling material."

"What about good husband material? Can
we spot that?"

"That wasn't one of the options. I guess
we're all on our own there."

"I'm not sure I like this study," said Margo,
who had been divorced before she met
Robert. "These researchers always seem to
come up with more and more ways to lay any
failure on women."

"Settle down." Rosie began to pass a photo
to each in the circle. "I'm sure they'll do a
study of what men read in women's faces, but
let's work with what they think they've discovered at the moment."

Bailey looked at the photo she'd been
handed and shook her head. "You go for the
strangest parlor games, Rosie. Where did you
get these photos?"

"I have an in at the university." That was
an understatement. A political creature,
Rosie had an *in* almost anywhere you could
think of. "Some of these photos are copies

from the original study. For those I've written the data on how they view children on the back. The others are from my family, and I've written some very subjective observations on the back of those. The rest are from magazines and the newspaper. These last guys are pure conjecture. Look closely, ladies. Reach back into your primal DNA and see if you can pick father or fling. And pass the photos around."

Selena looked at the photo of the stranger before her, but conjured an image of Drew's father instead. With him, she had known. Immediately. Despite the family photos he'd kept on his desk, he was a selfish bastard. Fit only for a fling. So why hadn't she been brought up short? Because she'd been young and self-absorbed and hadn't cared? Or worse, because she'd known he was only fling material, and it had suited her needs?

An only child, she'd always wanted a child of her own. And now she had Drew. Had it been a deliberate act?

What did that say about her?

The laughter of the group pierced her thoughts as Nora held up a photo of a man who must have been a model or an actor. Gorgeous. "Do we really care if he'll change diapers?"

Margo was looking at her photo. "This man has the most intense gaze. There's hurt in his eyes, but kindness, as well. I think he needs a family."

Rosie, who was circulating, looking over the others' shoulders, took Margo's photo and handed it to Selena. "What about this guy? I picked him out of a recent *Chronicle* article. Father material or fling?" she asked.

The face of Jack Quinn stared up at her.

This was too much.

Selena felt pushed beyond her limits. And here, of all places, where she'd always felt safe and accepted. Shoving the photo aside, she leapt from her seat and ran through the café, heedless of her friends' entreaties to come back. Outside, a steady drizzle had begun to fall, the weather matching her mood.

Everyone seemed to be pressuring her to *let go*. Of her haphazard dating style. Of her growing son. Of her perceptions of her parents.

Of her fears and insecurities.

Now where did that barbed postscript come from? Never a particularly introspective person, Selena had always considered herself fearless and secure. Now, nudged and prodded from all sides, she apparently had been turned topsy-turvy.

Rounding a corner, she stopped in her tracks. On an overpass directly ahead someone had painted *Give peace a chance*. Attached to the overpass were sixteen— exactly sixteen—whitewashed "doves" in flight, crude two-by-fours nailed at right angled *L*'s, now used as lopsided *V*'s. Her pilfered frames for the "Swan Song" wind harp. There was no mistake.

Great. In addition to being nudged, prodded and pressured by her friends, some rogue installation artist had made an end-run on her professional identity.

CHAPTER TEN

AFTER WORKING at his center with Axel for several hours, Jack had driven Drew home. He'd followed the boy up to the loft because he wanted to check once more on Selena's wrist. Although, Selena, the whole person, and her puzzling mental state were of some concern, as well. He still didn't have a handle on why she'd become so antagonistic.

On the landing, Drew unlocked and opened the loft door. "Looks like Mom fell asleep on the couch." With Axel he headed to the kitchen. On the way, he pushed the flashing light on the answering machine.

"Selena, pick up. It's Rosie. I deliberately chose that photo, yes. I thought the study would be a good framework to examine your feelings, but I didn't mean to upset you. I'm so sorry. Call me."

"It's Margo. Selena, are you okay? The group has decided to meet this Thursday at eight. An official meeting. So mark your calendar. Support is only five days away. But you know if you need to talk, you can drop in anytime."

"Selena, it's Nora. What happened? Was it us? Please, don't keep us in the dark."

"Bailey, here. I just want to say, we're not the enemy. We love you. You've got to know that. Derrick says to punch something, but I told him about your wrist. Anyway, he's just thinking like a guy…."

Drew didn't seem disturbed by the messages. "Mom's friends get pretty emotional at times," he said as he rummaged in the fridge. "Hey, we're out of bread and milk. I'm going to the corner store."

"I want to check your mom's wrist." Jack looked at the sofa where Selena, slumped against the cushions, hadn't moved during the replaying of the messages. "Maybe I can get her to go to bed where she'll be more comfortable."

"Axel and I'll be right back."

As the door closed, Jack moved toward

Selena. Only then did he see the half-empty bottle of cognac. When he knelt beside her, he discovered she wasn't asleep, but—just guessing by the smell of alcohol—very drunk. What the hell was going on?

"Selena? Are you okay?"

Her eyes fluttered open. "Jus' peachy."

"What happened today? Your friends sound concerned."

"Nothin' happened." She struggled to sit up, then flung her arms wide. "Ever'one's tellin' me to *let go,* so I did."

"I don't think this is what they had in mind." Drew didn't need to see his mother like this. Jack needed to get her cleaned up and in bed. Then a scary thought hit him. "Did you take anything besides the cognac? Besides the Advil?"

"Nope. Th'cognac was plenty. M'sieur Rémy Martin and I have become bes' buds. *Bons amis.*" Puckering up as if to kiss the bottle, she reached for it, but he snatched it away. "If the stuff was good enough for ol' Napoleon, i's good enough for me."

"Come on," he said. "Let's get you cleaned up. Then we'll get something in your stomach."

"You're tryin' to sober me up."

"You're quick." He didn't ask if this little binge was a one-off or a regular occurrence. There was a lot he didn't know about her.

He lifted her into his arms, then headed for the bathroom. Surprisingly, she didn't resist. Placing her on the closed toilet seat, he put toothpaste on her brush—at least he thought it was hers; it was neon pink with sparkles embedded in the plastic. "Brush," he commanded as he found a clean washcloth and ran the water until it was warm.

She leaned sideways and spit toward the sink. She missed. He now had toothpaste on his shirt.

"So sorry," she mumbled, trying to wipe the paste off, but smearing it instead. The toothbrush clattered into the sink. She swayed unsteadily, but he was ready and caught her, although not before she wiped her mouth on his already pasty shirt.

She kicked her legs straight out in front of her. "Iss the room spinning?"

"No. But keep your feet on the floor. It'll help ground you."

She did as he said. Mistrusting her new

biddable nature, he held her still and washed her face. Brushed her hair. Lifted her in his arms again and made for her bedroom. At least she now smelled slightly better.

He arranged pillows behind her so she could sit up, but when he pulled away, she wrapped her arms around his neck.

"Don' go." Her voice was unusually husky.

"I'm not. I'm just going to make you some toast and coffee. Drew's gone to buy bread and milk."

She didn't release him. "I don' wan' toas' an' coffee. I wan' us to clear the air."

"You're talking about what's bothering you?"

"Yesh."

"And that would be?"

"You."

"I kind of figured that, but I don't know what I've done. That makes it difficult for me to make amends."

She ran her fingers through his hair. "Sleep with me."

"As in close our eyes so you can sleep off the cognac?"

"No. As in hot and heavy sex."

He had to admit the idea had crossed his mind on more than one occasion, but now was definitely not one of them. If they made love, he didn't want alcohol doing the wanting for her. He tried to untangle her fingers. "Selena..."

"Do you know what it does to me when you say my name?"

"You have a beautiful name."

"Then sleep with me and my beautiful name. Jus' once." Her hands slipped from his neck to cover her eyes. "So we can break this damn tension. This stupid attraction." She started to weep. "So we can get over it and move on."

He didn't know about her, but, for him, sleeping with her wasn't going to make him get over her. He kissed her lightly on her forehead. "You'll feel better once you have something in your stomach."

"Jus' like a man. The way to his heart is through my stomach."

No. It was her heart they were talking about, and he doubted a bellyful of toast was going to cure whatever ache she—or he—was feeling. Just the same, he headed for the kitchen with a detour to the sofa to retrieve the cognac bottle. To put it away before Drew got home.

Too late. Drew stepped through the door with Axel. "What's that?"

"Your mother had a drink too many on an empty stomach—"

"She drank half a bottle of that? She never drinks more than a couple glasses of wine. This stuff came in a gift basket from one of her sponsors. I never saw her touch it." A worried expression on his face, the boy looked toward the empty sofa. "Is she okay?"

"She will be when she gets something to eat. I was going to make coffee. How about you make toast."

"I...I could do that." Frowning, Drew moved into the kitchen, dumped his purchases on the butcher's block and retrieved butter, a knife and a plate. "She doesn't usually drink. Honest."

Making coffee, Jack didn't respond.

"You're not going to call Social Services, are you?"

"I'm not going to call Social Services. I think your mom's been feeling a little pressure lately. The injury to her wrist just topped everything off. If she's not used to drinking much, well, cognac can pack a punch even in small doses."

That explanation didn't seem to comfort Drew. "What kind of pressure?"

"I'm not sure really. She only hinted at it."

"Maybe…maybe me talking about my father?"

"No. That wouldn't do it." Not alone, at least. As one in a line of dominoes, probably. But Drew didn't need a guilt trip. "Adults worry. About everything. That's what they do." And so, it seemed, did kids.

"The toast is ready," Drew said. "Is the coffee?"

"Just about."

"Can I take them to her?"

"Sure. Before you do, would you write Maxine's number down for me?"

"Yeah. But you don't have to call her. She stops in at least twice a day. Today she'll wanna tell Mom about her date." Jack was glad to see some of the tension had drained from Drew's voice. He looked directly at Jack. "My mom's a real good mom. She's always taken great care of me. I just wanna be clear on that."

"We're clear. I think her friends want her to take great care of herself, too." He poured a mug of freshly brewed coffee.

"Are you coming?" Drew asked, picking up the mug and the plate of toast.

"No. If Maxine will be by later, I'll leave. You have my number if you need anything."

He watched the boy head for his mother's room, the caregiver roles reversed.

Like Drew, Jack worried about the part he'd played in pushing Selena to the edge. When the hangover cleared, she'd still want Drew around. She'd want Maxine and the women he'd heard on the answering machine around. He'd feel a hell of a lot better if he thought she'd want him around.

SHE'D MADE a complete ass of herself.

And for the past few days Selena's most important job had been trying to make amends. Sunday she'd poured the cognac down the sink as Drew watched. She'd told him pain had made her overindulge. That hadn't been a lie. But the pain hadn't been physical. Her wrist had been the least of it.

She told him she'd been wrong, had set a bad example and she was sorry.

Then she'd called each of her friends to apologize. She'd told them she'd try to explain in detail, if they still wanted to listen, Thursday evening.

Monday she'd picked up a huge gift basket of assorted Sees candies to bring to the meeting. That had been a mistake. By the look of the open boxes—especially the empty peanut brittle box—she should have waited till Thursday to pick up the peace offering. Cut out the booze, bring on the sweets. What was wrong with her self-control lately?

Tuesday she'd relented and called in extra interns to help Maxine set up the tolerance installation at the university. As difficult as it had been not to get physically involved, she'd coddled her injured wrist and maintained a supervisory role. And avoided her mentor's questioning looks. No prude, Maxine wouldn't have given her grief about the lapse into drunkenness. What she might have worried about—although she hadn't said— was Selena's state of mind that precipitated the binge. Mind? Hah! What mind?

The one person she hadn't dealt with was Quinn.

Wednesday afternoon, Selena sat in Drew's school gymnasium, which had been set up as a giant career fair. Booths had been erected for various occupations, and parents in those occupations manned the booths, talked to students, provided hands-on activities and passed out literature. A staging area with audience seating had been set at one end of the room for demonstrations. In past years Selena had done her thing on the stage. With slide shows, scavenged materials and audience participation, she'd been proud to be known as Drew's mother and an artist. Now she sat in the audience as Drew and Quinn prepared to give their presentation.

Quinn, the interloper.

She hadn't seen or heard from him since Saturday. Normally, silence from a guy in her life wouldn't phase her, but she had a vague recollection she'd propositioned Quinn. And that he'd refused her. She didn't know which act shocked her more.

Today he'd driven to the school on his own, and, while she'd been finding a seat, she'd seen him signing in at the presenters' table and hooking up with Drew. She hadn't had an opportunity to speak to him. She wasn't looking forward to the moment when she did.

Breathe, she told herself, *and enjoy your child's presentation. Let go.*

As the principal introduced Drew and Quinn, Selena noticed for the first time that her son held his head a little higher than usual, his shoulders a little straighter. He might still be small for his age, but in the past three weeks he'd acquired an air of assurance. Of maturity. He'd taken a step into adulthood, and his stature had increased. As much as she hated admitting it, Quinn had played a big part in the transformation.

The middle school students in the audience were still chattering as Quinn began to speak into the mike, but they quieted almost immediately when Drew brought Axel on stage. Even in a huge gymnasium the dog looked enormous. Formidable. What beastmaster could tame him? That unspoken question hung in the air and pulled in the young audience. From Drew and Axel's entrance on, the kids sat up and paid attention as Quinn spoke and Drew confidently put Axel through his well-practiced paces. Once again she noticed how Quinn stepped back and let her son take center stage.

Drew put Axel through basic dog-handling techniques, then progressed to Axel carrying and pulling loads, then on to some agility exercises, and finished with some tricks designed purely as crowd pleasers. She was surprised to see Drew pull helpers from the audience, and even more surprised that he only picked girls. Her boy was growing up in more ways than one. At the end of the demonstration, the applause was thunderous. Classmates crowded around Drew to pet Axel and ask questions. Pride made Selena's eyes moist. So intent was she on watching her son, she didn't see Quinn approach.

"Hello, Selena."

She actually jumped. "Quinn! Well, I…I have to admit you've proven your expertise with dogs, but…you might also know a thing or two about adolescent boys."

"Thank you."

Drew, his face flushed with triumph, approached, leading Axel and trailing a group of appreciative classmates. For the very first time— ever—she wondered if having a parenting partner might have had its merits.

"I'm so proud of you!" she said, opening her arms.

"Mom! Ix-nay on the ug-hay!" But he grinned. "Axel had a ball! Didn't you, boy?"

"I'd say Axel is a born ham," Quinn commented. "Can I interest you two superstars— and superstars' mom, of course—in ice cream as soon as you're dismissed? I saw a place within walking distance. My treat."

"You two go without us," Drew replied. "Angel Diaz asked me to come over to her house for a couple hours before supper. She has two rescue greyhounds. And, yes, her grandmother's going to be home. Here's her number." He held out his hand, where he'd scribbled the phone number in ink on his palm, long enough for Selena to copy it into her cell phone. "I gotta go meet up with my homeroom for dismissal."

So Quinn and she were on their own.

As they made their way through the crowd, there was no need for conversation, but as the crowd thinned outside the building, she sensed Quinn was waiting for her to make the first move.

"I…I just wanted to tell you," she said, walking in the direction of the little ice cream parlor he'd mentioned. "I don't usually make it a habit to get drunk on Saturday afternoon. Or any other afternoon for that matter. I'm strictly a two-glass gal."

"Drew told me. He wanted me to understand you were a good mother."

"He said that? You're not extrapolating? Trying to make the drunken sot feel better?"

"I think his exact words were, 'My mom's a real good mom. She's always taken great care of me.'"

"Wow. That's good to know."

"You sound surprised."

"I feel like I've been a good mom. But lately Drew's been so moody, so closed into himself I wonder what's going on in that brain of his. He's nothing if not a constant surprise."

Quinn walked next to her, but she sensed he was still waiting.

"I want to thank you for your help," she said. "I know you probably knew all along that if Drew gained control over that loveable mutt, he'd gain some control over himself. I failed to see that."

"Sometimes you can't see what's too close. But now that you know, it'll be your job to see Drew maintains control. Just like teenagers, dogs can destabilize in unpredictable situations. Having a pet requires consistency of leadership."

"Not so far different from parenthood." A month ago she'd never have expected that comment to come out of her mouth. Like some forgotten wit, she'd always thought consistency the hobgoblin of little minds.

Quinn stopped at the ice cream parlor's take-out window. "What's your pleasure?"

She could have said *this*. A mild February day. A son to be proud of. And…a friend to share the experience with. It would be nice, she suddenly realized, if she and Quinn could be friends. It would help dim the building sexual electricity she always felt in his presence.

"Rocky Road," she said instead.

They took their cones—she, not surprised he chose a deceptively simple green-tea ice cream—and sat on a bench, for a while content to take in the mosaic of city life around them. The sidewalk vendor selling yucca flowers. The moms and dads in jogging outfits, pushing expensive "exercise" strollers past the anime mural that heralded bicycle and skateboard activism. The people streaming in and out of the cramped independent bookstore that sold kites as well. And, as always, a mix of music drifting out of a café or apartment windows.

She felt Quinn watching her.

"Yoda me this," she said, the love of her surroundings easing her guardedness. "How can you manage dozens of unrelated dogs while I seem to be having difficulty with one twelve-year-old boy I've known since birth."

"Humans aren't pack animals. We're all individuals. With different wants and needs. And kids aren't clones of their parents. That's the challenge. And the satisfaction. Drew's going to be okay. So are you."

"When he moves on." She felt a little sad, even with the prospect of his going in the distant future. She wanted time to stand still.

"You wouldn't have raised him right if he

didn't want to move on." Quinn used his paper napkin to wipe the tip of her nose. "A direct hit. If Axel were here, he'd have taken care of it."

"You lie," she replied. "I'm a fastidious eater. Rarely need a napkin." With the banter she felt any tension that might have been between them lessen.

"So where do you see yourself when Drew's on his own? You'd be free to move beyond San Francisco. Take your work to a wider stage. Would you like that?"

"I always thought so, but now I don't know. I love it here. This is a home that suits me. Although, having the wrist out of commission, I've wondered if I might be happier giving up the installations themselves to begin a mentoring program based in the city. Where artists from around the world could come to learn my concepts, techniques and funding strategies. To brainstorm their own. To create a center full of synergy. That might be the next step. I don't know. Although my friends are all urging me to think about the next step, I'm a person who's always tried to live in the moment. And I don't react well to being pushed."

"Is that what the date with Rémy Martin and the phone messages were all about?"

"Partly." She didn't want to talk about herself any more. "So, how about you? Do you know what you want, or do you already have it?"

It took him a while to answer.

"Five years ago," he finally said, "after the death of my wife—Anneka—I would have said all I wanted was to lose myself in the world of animals. Now…I realize that the good marriage I had makes me want another strong connection." He looked her directly in the eyes. "I'm content in my present life, but to be honest, I want someone to share it. And not just in a superficial way."

Selena sensed she was stepping into a minefield, but she had to ask. "So you want to marry again?"

"Yes. Eventually."

"I don't. Definitely not. I've always been a loner. A loner who likes intermittent contact with people, mind you. I don't see why we can't just ebb and flow in and out of each others' lives. Like the tide. Besides, the divorce statistics are outrageous, making me wonder what's the advantage to a piece of paper and a promise of permanence."

"Is that how you see marriage? A piece of paper and a promise?"

She thought for a minute of her friends. Progressively paired off. Clearly, they saw something more in the institution. Perhaps, if you'd always been on the outside looking in, as she had been, her way was the safe way. Look but don't touch. That way nothing got broken.

"My friends seem happy," she said. "But so am I."

He stood. "I've got to get back to the center."

"Would you like to join Drew and me for supper?"

"What would the point be? Axel's trained."

"I...I'd like us to be friends."

"I have enough friends," he replied. "I'd hoped we could be more."

In silence he walked her back to the school and her car.

CHAPTER ELEVEN

ON THURSDAY EVENING, for the first time, Selena felt uneasy approaching her coffee house friends. They were all assembled ahead of her—Margo, Nora, Derrick, Bailey and Rosie—in the annex, which glowed with candlelight and camaraderie. Holding the "peace" basket of Sees candies—she'd had to replace most of the plundered boxes—she stood a little outside the meeting room before the others noticed her.

Derrick was first. "Selena! Are you going to play statue all night, or are you going to get in here? Bailey has pictures of our day at Fisherman's Wharf. Acting like tourists."

"That was weeks ago."

"I keep forgetting to bring the laptop," Bailey replied, setting up the slide show on the low table so that everyone could see.

Glad for the distraction, Selena put her candy basket on a table in the corner, then settled in to watch photos of Derrick and Bailey, their two girls and Rosie's son mugging for the camera. A blended—really, an extended—family, they looked as if they were having a ball. Is that how her little group had looked at the beginning of the Midnight Rollers excursion? She'd been so tense she hadn't let herself fully enjoy the experience. Had let a lovely Kodak moment slip by until her fall had put the whammy on the whole outing.

"Omigosh!" Rosie exclaimed. "I know those photos were taken only a few weeks ago, but I think all three kids have grown an inch."

"The clothing budget confirms it."

"Time flies."

"So enjoy every second."

Time did fly. And what had Selena been doing with her precious fleeting moments these last weeks? Resisting them. Squandering them in stubbornness. Treating them as if they were something to be gotten through until she could get her life back to normal. Until she could get her own way. She found herself gulping back tears and couldn't remember a time in her life when she'd been so emotional.

"Selena, do you need some water?" Nora asked.

"No, thank you. Just give me a minute."

Concerned looks on their faces, the others nonetheless returned to their conversation.

"We had so much fun that day," Bailey said. "Leslie and Savannah loved playing big sisters to Casey."

"Spoiling him, you mean," Rosie replied. "He came home, thinking he was the crown prince."

"As if Hud doesn't treat him like the crown prince."

"You got me there."

Margo left the room and came back with a fabulous chocolate layer cake. "Ellie's been bugging me about getting all our kids together. She hears us down here—" Margo and Robert lived above the café "—and says the adults get to have all the fun…."

The voices seemed to hang in the air above Selena. For how long, she couldn't tell.

"Milano!" Derrick said, waving his hand

in front of her face. "Are you ready to tell us why you've been acting crazier than usual?"

"And whether this is for us," Rosie added, eyeing the Sees candies.

"The basket is for all of you, yes. For putting up with me. I know I've been acting nuts—"

"Nuttier."

"Nuttier. And I might have thrown a scare into the group. It's just that…you were right. In trying to get me to be honest. About my feelings. That's never been easy for me to do."

"Your feelings about Jack Quinn?"

"Yes."

"And we were right. You are attracted to him."

"Yes."

"Hooray!" Nora exclaimed. "Let the relationship begin!"

Everyone applauded, but Selena held up her hands. "It's not that easy."

Derrick looked suspicious. "What have you done to the man?"

Selena recounted yesterday's conversation with Quinn. "I might be attracted to him, but don't you think he's moving too fast? Pushing too hard?"

"Because he wants to be more than friends?" Rosie asked. "Because he can see the possibility of a relationship ending in marriage?"

"Hey, I've just admitted I'm attracted to him."

"You made the admission to us. Does he know?"

"Perhaps…not really…no. So don't you think he's jumping the gun a bit, issuing this relationship ultimatum?" She looked to Derrick for a man's reading of the situation.

"It's a big man who can admit what he really wants," he said. "Especially if it runs against stereotype. Obviously, he values a serious relationship. You've got to give him props for honesty."

"That means I should just fall into marriage? Skip dating, courtship, fun and games or whatever tag people want to hang on the unencumbered part?"

"I don't think that's at all what he's asking you to do," Margo replied. "He's asking you to treat your relationship—should you choose to pursue one—with care. To be open to the possibility it might get serious. Might even last."

"How scary is that!"

"Selena!" Bailey looked shocked. "You've met a man who freely admits he's not afraid of commitment and you're tossing him away?"

"He kind of did the tossing."

"No. He left the final decision to you. The power, Selena. He *gave* you the power to say yes or no. I want to meet this man."

Margo pulled an address book from her apron. "And if you don't want him, I know a dozen women who'd take your place in a heartbeat."

"Let's not go overboard."

"Oh, ho!" Derrick crowed. "I think they call that attitude dog-in-the-manger!"

Selena felt a little guilty. She wasn't sure she was ready for a serious adult relationship, but she sure as hell didn't want other women trying Quinn on for size. "Isn't there a dating injured reserve list?"

Margo reached over to lay her hand atop Selena's. "Do yourself a favor and call him. It's great you can be open with us, but he's the one you should be discussing all this with."

Easier said than done. Why did life's choices seem to get progressively more complicated?

She looked at her friends, who were looking at her. Waiting.

"Have you noticed," she asked, "that I've taken up an inordinate chunk of group time lately? I mean, why does my life seem so unsettled and yours seem so serene?"

"I wouldn't exactly call my life serene," Margo said, "but compared to ten months ago, it has improved dramatically."

The group members gave each other little uneasy glances.

"What?" Selena asked. "What are you keeping from me?"

"We're not keeping anything from you, hon," Nora said. "It's just that it's so obvious."

"Then what am I not seeing?"

"Life is still life," Rosie replied. "A hectic carnival ride, but…"

"But?"

"But it's not as stressful," Rosie said, looking for all the world as if she didn't want to have to spell it out if Selena couldn't already see it, "because we're not single parents anymore. Two people shouldering the pressures of family life sure beats the heck out of going it alone."

Selena looked around the group. Every single—no, not single, part-of-a-pair— member was nodding in agreement. And each looked a little sheepish, as if this was a special secret revealed only to couples.

Her parents knew this secret. They lived it. Yet they'd urged their daughter not to cling. To be strong. To forge a singular path. They'd intimated that the path of self-reliance was the path to happiness. But perhaps—and this thought was a new and disturbing one—it was Selena herself who'd interpreted their teachings as *emotional* self-reliance. Perhaps she had only herself to blame for her stubborn resistance to relationships of substance.

Margo knelt next to her chair and gave her a heartfelt hug. "Would a big piece of chocolate cake help?"

It couldn't hurt.

THIS WAS WHEN he'd usually go into seclusion.

But, having felt alive for the past month,

Jack refused to crawl back into a self-imposed isolation because Selena thought she wanted to be just friends. If he never saw her again, he should thank his lucky stars she'd ever crossed his path. Had drawn him back into the world of people and emotion. Corny as it sounded, his life had gone from black-and-white to Technicolor. Because of her. A month ago he'd asked himself if he could love a woman like Selena. The answer was, he did.

So, he wasn't giving up on her. He simply needed to give her space to let her think. In the meantime, he devoted his time to his dogs, to his clients and to his staff. Actually, his new friendliness seemed to scare the crap out of his employees. Even Andy had asked, "What's up, boss? You on something?"

Ted had wondered, too, since Jack had called to ask him to run the Coastal Trail on Sunday with the dogs. "I don't see you for three months," his brother had said, "and now I see you three times in two weeks? What gives?"

Now Jack stood at the counter of the pet supply store, working with the owner to put together a special gift basket of dog biscuits,

chew toys and a new leash. He'd created a
diploma on his computer and a graduation
card, both made out to Axel and bearing an
official-looking seal with his center's logo.
Both bogus, but Selena didn't have to know
this wasn't the usual culmination of completed sessions. Didn't need to know that in
all the time he'd been in business, he'd never
done something so silly. When the basket
was finished to his satisfaction, he gave the
woman the Milanos' address.

Sure, he'd walked away from Selena. But
he couldn't forget her, and he wasn't about
to let her forget him.

LATE MONDAY AFTERNOON Selena arrived
home after errands to discover a note taped
to her apartment door. *Attempted delivery.
Package left at produce market.* She didn't
mind a side trip to Sam's. She could check
up on Drew, who'd been making after-school
deliveries for the greengrocer for the past
week. She knew Sam wouldn't send her son
anywhere iffy, and she knew Axel would act
his protector, but it never hurt to check.
Because she also knew with a bittersweet

certainty Drew no longer shared every aspect of his life with her. Like that jar under his bed, filled with coins and labeled *Angel's birthday fund.*

So down to Sam's she went.

"That's quite a turnabout your kid and his mutt have made," Sam admitted, offering her an apple. "Who would've guessed a month ago he'd be one of my best employees?"

"He's your only employee, Sam. But I'm glad it's working out. Now, what's this about a package?"

"You're looking at it."

The only thing besides the register on Sam's spotless counter was a beautiful gift basket with an enormous plaid bow. On second glance, Selena could see it wasn't a fruit basket, but filled with doggie goodies. The envelope of the attached card was made out to Axel.

Sam grinned.

"Who delivered this?"

"The sign on the van said Gervase's Pet Supply. Aren't you going to open the card?"

Although intrigued, she said, "I think I'll take it upstairs and let Drew do the honors. When's his last delivery?"

"He's on it. He shouldn't be long. I'll send him up as soon as he gets back. Maybe that dog trainer Drew can't stop talking about sent you this."

"You didn't look inside the envelope, did you?"

Sam looked toward the ceiling. "Maybe the delivery guy mentioned who sent it. Or maybe I just thought it was the kind of thing this dog fellow would do. He seemed nice when we talked. Real considerate. The tall, quiet type women go for. You know, with their own hair, and all. Not only is he good with animals—which tells you something about his character—he's good with your son, Selena."

Matchmakers. The world was filled with incurable matchmakers.

She picked up the basket. "The gift's addressed to our dog, Sam. Thanks for accepting delivery."

"Anytime," Sam called out as she retreated. "A more predictable guy would have chosen flowers...."

Point taken. Sam had been her neighbor long enough to know how she disdained predictability.

As she stepped onto the sidewalk, the heavens opened up. Rain pelted the sidewalk. Running the short distance to her apartment entrance, she hoped Drew was close to home. Rush hour and rain were a dangerous mix.

Inside the loft, she set the basket on the butcher's block in the kitchen. Her heart thumped a little more quickly and not from climbing the stairs. This was from Quinn. Or was it from the center? A business follow-up engineered by Andy or another staff member who didn't even know her? She hadn't seen or talked to Quinn for five days, and, despite her friends' urgings, she found herself in uncharted territory and hesitant to make the initial contact. She touched the crinkly cellophane covering the basket like a child pressing its hands to a candy store window. Was this Quinn's way of reaching out?

Curiosity getting the better of her, she noted the envelope to the card was not sealed shut. What would it hurt to read the card, then return it and leave the "official" basket opening to Drew? Before she could give in to impulse, she heard a sickening screech of tires from the street below. Then raised voices.

The rain sluicing down the windows made it difficult to make out the particulars of the disturbance below. But the headlights of cars stopped at crazy angles revealed people racing toward the blurry but inert forms of a person and a very large dog lying still—too still—in the middle of the street.

CHAPTER TWELVE

Noooo! Not Drew, not Drew, not Drew!

Searing body and mind, the anguish rose within her as Selena flew down the stairs. She was a bad, bad mother. She should never have allowed Drew to make deliveries for Sam. She should have waited for her son just now instead of letting a stupid gift basket draw her upstairs and into thoughts of Jack Quinn. She should have concentrated on her child. On keeping him safe.

Sirens wailed in the distance. On the street she pushed through the rain-soaked crowd to an inner circle shielding Sam, who knelt on the street and wrapped a blanket around a crumpled form.

Selena felt her heart break. "Drew?"

"No, Charlie," Sam replied, gently tucking a jacket under the homeless man's bloodied head. Only now did she notice Charlie's shopping cart overturned in the street, the man's entire worldly possessions scattered and trampled. "I called 911."

"Mom!" The one word, choked with tears, was unmistakable. Drew. But where was he? Not in the faces of the crowd pressing closer. "Mom! He's not moving!"

She whirled about, searching for her son. Where was her son?

And who was not moving?

"I didn't see them!" a woman nearby cried. "They just stepped off the curb in front of me! I couldn't stop fast enough!"

The other voices, the headlights, the rain disoriented Selena. "Drew!"

"Come quick! Mom, pleeeease!"

In a panic, she brushed aside bystanders to follow her son's voice. There he sat in the gutter in the rain, cradling the lifeless form of a very large dog.

It took her a second to realize it wasn't Axel, but Charlie's dog, Pip.

At a distance Axel paced through the crowd, whining, his tail between his legs, ears back, his whole body shaking.

Selena threw her arms around Drew.

"We were in Sam's store," he sobbed, not letting go of Pip. "We saw Charlie step in front of the car!"

Charlie lived wrapped in his own private universe. Neither sun nor fog nor rain made any difference to him.

"What's he gonna do without Pip?" Drew wailed. Nearby, Axel set up an echoing howl.

Not wanting to say Charlie might not be any better off than Pip, Selena moved to shield her son from the sight of police clearing a path for the ambulance technicians. But it wasn't long before a police officer stood before their own little huddled threesome.

"Is anyone hurt here?"

"Ch-Charlie's dog!" Drew had begun to shake. "I th-think he's…" He couldn't say it.

"Son, we'll take care of the dog." The officer gently removed Pip from Drew's embrace, then looked at Selena. "Is this your son?"

She nodded, rain hiding the tears streaming down her face.

"You need to get him inside, ma'am."

When she pulled Drew to his feet, he slumped against her. Axel appeared from out of the crowd and crept beside them as they made their way back to the loft.

Glancing over her shoulder, Selena saw Charlie being lifted into the ambulance, an oxygen mask strapped over his face. "Charlie's alive," she assured Drew.

"But Pip was all Charlie had."

And you're all I have, Selena thought, feeling guilty that she felt overwhelming relief in the midst of another's misfortune.

Upstairs, she knew her son had been badly shaken when he let her hover. She ran the shower for him till it was hot, then laid out fresh towels. While he showered and the kettle simmered for hot chocolate, she tried to towel-dry Axel, who seemed as traumatized as her son. Unaccountably, he growled at her when she tried to wipe down his hindquarters. Was he hurt, too? Although it had been a week and a half since she'd injured her wrist skating, she didn't want to chance reinjuring it, strong-arming a hundred-pound dog into doing her bidding. A little extra damp in the apartment wouldn't hurt anything. And surely she'd be able to tell by his walk if he was ailing. When she let him go, he slunk off to Drew's bedroom. No limp, but no pizzazz, either. Clearly, all was not well in the universe, and Axel sensed it, too.

On Tuesday, Drew awoke with a cold and asked to stay home from school. He also made Selena promise to get a status report on Charlie. When she went into the kitchen to make breakfast, she discovered Axel had been into the basket Quinn had sent. He'd strewn the contents—those that he hadn't eaten—throughout the loft. He'd also relieved himself on the floor in her studio.

Maxine checked in and insisted she make the necessary contacts to postpone all instal-lation work for a few days. She urged Selena to get Drew to talk about his feelings.

Easier said than done.

Although Drew insisted on taking Axel outside for the necessary pit stops, he didn't walk his dog. And when the two returned to the apartment, they both climbed back in bed. Axel ate little. Drew ate less.

Drew didn't want to talk.

She called Sam, who told her Charlie had scrapes and bruises and a broken arm. The free-clinic personnel had set the arm and released Charlie back onto the street. He hadn't shown up in the district again, but Sam was setting up a fund jar for him, in case. Selena told Drew Charlie had been released from the hospital. The news only seemed to make Drew sadder. He clung to Axel.

Early Wednesday morning, when Selena tried to enter Drew's bedroom to see if he felt up to going to school, a growling Axel barred the way. As she brushed by him, he nipped her on the calf, drawing blood.

That did it.

She could deal with a grieving boy, or she could deal with an unstable dog, but she couldn't deal with both. And her son was her top priority.

Whether she wanted him or not, she needed Quinn to deal with the dog.

HE WENT TO HER apartment as soon as she called. Without waiting for her to explain the need over the phone. Her tone of voice told him this was an emergency. When she finally related what happened, he knew he could help.

"Will you take Axel to your center?" she

asked as they stood in her kitchen. Her eyes red and rimmed with dark circles, she made coffee for the two of them. "Just for a while. Until Drew feels better. I don't know why he's turned on me. Axel, that is."

"His pack leader's down. The way Axel sees it, if someone doesn't assume the position, he's going to have to take over—"

"Please, stop." Wearily, she held up her hand. "I can't cope with the dog psychology right now. I just need you to take Axel while Drew heals."

"I can't."

"Won't, you mean. I thought you said you'd help. I'll pay you."

"I'm not going to take your money. I'm trying to explain healing's not possible for either boy or dog if you separate them. Now, especially. Drew empathizes so deeply with Charlie's loss, it would traumatize him even further to have his own dog taken away."

"But it would only be temporary. I'd explain."

"You can't explain to Axel. And right now, in his unstable state, he needs a firm leader."

"You want me to make Drew get out of bed

to put Axel through his paces? Now, when they're both hurting?" Her eyes flashed anger. "You might know dogs, but clearly, you've never been a parent."

He had to remind himself that she, too, was speaking from hurt. "Drew needs his dog. He also needs his mother. Axel needs a leader. You're going to have to fill that role, as well."

"I thought you told us when Axel accepted Drew as leader, he'd accept me, too." She turned her leg to show the bandage on her calf. "Well, he bit me. Some show of respect."

"When a dog's world destabilizes, anything goes. It doesn't mean we can't restore the natural order. But if you let Axel get away with this dominant behavior, you're inviting more trouble down the road."

"Gawd, I just wanted a little help."

"I'm trying to give it to you. And if you'd stop fighting me, we could take care of this with a walk."

"You and your damned walks."

"They work. Get the leash. I'm going to talk to Drew."

"I can take care of my son. I want you to take care of the dog."

Ignoring her, he walked into the boy's room without speaking. Moved slowly toward the growling dog without making eye contact. Backed him into a corner and stood over him as Drew watched silently from his bed. Within seconds, Axel's whole demeanor became one of calm submission. Someone putting a human spin on it might think he seemed relieved to have responsibility lifted from him.

Jack sat on the edge of Drew's bed. "It's hard to lose a loved one. I know."

"How do you know?"

A boy with such depths of empathy was old enough to get an honest answer. Jack swallowed hard. "My wife, Anneka, died. Five years ago. She was very sick."

Drew's eyes welled up with tears. "I'm sorry."

"Thank you. But I'm not telling you to make you feel worse. I'm telling you that it's not the end of the world. Although I thought it was at the time."

"I keep thinking of Charlie. If he loved

Pip half as much as I love Axel—" Drew's voice broke.

"He feels awful now, yes."

"What's gonna happen to him?"

"I don't know. I don't know Charlie's story. Why he's on the street. Hopefully, he'll recover from his physical injuries. If he does, I bet he'll find another dog. A stray who needs Charlie as much as Charlie needs him."

"People living on the street. Car accidents. Losing the ones you love. I wish things didn't have to be this way."

Jack did, too. But he had enough years under his belt to realize one often could only effect small improvements.

"Your mom's worried about you. And so's Axel."

"I know. He bit her."

"Why do you think he did?"

"Maybe he's picking up on my bad energy."

"Maybe you're a really bright kid." He laid a hand on the boy's shoulder. He seemed so fragile. But who wasn't underneath? "You need to concentrate on getting rid of this cold. In the meantime, I'm going to teach your mother how to take over as pack leader."

That last statement coaxed a wan smile from the patient. "What do you say, Mom?"

Jack turned to see Selena standing in the door, leash in hand, an inscrutable expression on her face, making him wonder how much of the conversation she'd heard.

He rose. "Walk up to Axel as if you mean business," he told her. "No sweet talk. No asking permission. Just snap on the leash. You're in charge, and he needs to know it."

She did as he said. Even issued a sharp, "Hut!" when the dog began to whine. Jack suspected she was imagining he was the one on the other end of the leash.

"Now we're going for a walk," he said.

Selena shot him a glance as sharp as the order she'd given Axel, then turned to Drew. "Maxine's supposed to be by in a little bit. We won't be long, though."

"Make him sit at the door, Mom," Drew said. "Then you go through the door first."

"Listen to your son. He knows what he's talking about."

"Orders," she muttered. "My life has devolved into taking orders." But she seemed relieved at the promise things might return to normal.

At the door to the stairs, she made Axel sit. "If you're coming," she said to Jack, "I assume you'll be *following*, as well."

Glad to see some of her spirit returning, he let the challenge slide.

On the sidewalk she managed Axel efficiently, but Jack sensed she needed to get something off her chest.

"Is this enough walking?" she asked after a few minutes.

"No. He's still anxious. We need to wear him out. You'll know by his body language when it's okay to bring him home."

"We might be out here all morning."

"I doubt it, but is that a bad thing? Seems like you could use some focused exercise, too."

She didn't look at him. "Why did you tell Drew about your wife when you've never told me?"

"I talk about Anneka with very few people."

"That doesn't answer my question."

"How to explain when I'm not even sure I know the answer?"

"Try."

"If you'd told me a month ago I'd be confiding in a twelve-year-old kid, I'd have said you were crazy. But there's a connection with Drew. A connection acknowledging loss that a lot of adults shy away from making. I know I have. But with Drew there's an openness, an honesty. First about sharing his sense of loss in never knowing his biological father. Then in his empathy, his grief, for Charlie and the loss of his dog. Maybe it's Drew, or maybe it's just kids who don't hold back. As I've been doing. I think their way's healthier. Maybe in Drew's presence I feel safe enough to explore my own feelings of loss. Does this make any sense?"

"Y-yes." A short distance into the park, she stopped walking. Stood looking off into the distance, her back to him. Suddenly, her shoulders started to shake. And she began to weep. Uncontrollably.

He pulled her to him.

"I thought it was Drew in the street," she cried. "With Axel. For a few horrifying minutes, I thought I'd lost my son."

Axel whined. Holding Selena in a one-armed embrace, Jack took the leash from her hand, clicked it sharply and made the dog lie at their feet.

Selena sobbed into the front of his jacket. "I don't know what I would have done if…if…"

"Don't think of the *ifs* now. Drew's safe."

"Omigod, I've tried to be strong in front of him, but it's been so hard."

"You're not in front of him now. Let it all out."

With his free hand he stroked her hair, her back, and let her lean into him. Let her tears soak his jacket until there were no more tears. Until she snuffled and looked up at him.

"You…you wouldn't have a tissue, would you?"

He fumbled in his pocket and came up with a clean paper napkin from a sub shop.

"Thanks." When she blew her nose, she honked like a goose, and he found it difficult not to smile. "You know I've never even cried in front of Maxine."

"Believe me, I won't tell her."

"Your brother says you and I are alike."

"How so?"

"Says we both tend to hide our pain."

"I'm not so sure anymore that's a good thing."

"But it's scary showing yourself as vulnerable."

"It shouldn't be scary if you trust the person you reveal yourself to." He wanted to pull her back into his arms, but she seemed rooted to the ground. "You can trust me, Selena."

"Do you know what is so unbelievable?" She took a deep breath, and her whole body shuddered. "I want to trust you…but I don't know how."

He reached for her then. Only held out his free arm for her to step into his embrace. She did. Holding him as tightly as he held her.

"You've already given trust a start," he said. "You trusted your dog to me. You invited me into your home. You've trusted me with your son. All that's left is you. And the flip side of the coin. Can I trust you?"

Her hands still on his waist, she moved back slightly to look at him, a puzzled expression on her face. "Why wouldn't you trust me?"

"You fascinate me, Selena, but I'm not one

of your college boys. I've been around the block a few times, and I've learned something about myself. I'm not interested in games. And I sure as hell don't want someone toying with my emotions."

"I...wouldn't do that."

"Not deliberately, no. But you might pull back if things looked like they were getting serious."

"Do you think things could get serious between us?"

He thought they already were, but he wasn't about to admit it. Instead, he kissed her, and kissed her as if she needed convincing. Kissed her until he felt a hard desire rising. Until she whimpered and clung to him. Until he had to break away before he suggested they go to his place. Now. For the rest of the day. So that he could show her just how serious he was.

"If that's how you get earthlings onto the Mother Ship," she panted, "it's a damned good plan."

Glad to see the old Selena reemerging, he ran with the moment. "Come away with me," he urged, trying to catch his own breath.

"To the Mother Ship?"

"No." He kissed the top of her head, inhaled the scent of her. "To the Mayacamas Mountains where I have a cabin. For a weekend. This weekend."

"Just the two of us?"

"Not even a dog in sight."

"To see just how serious we might get."

"Yes."

"Beyond friendship."

"Beyond friendship."

Her expression clouded. "I've never been away from Drew."

"I'm sure Maxine would stay with him."

"She would. That's not the issue."

"What is?"

"What do I tell Drew?"

"The truth." He let his hands slide down her arms to interlock their fingers. "If you want separate sleeping arrangements, separate sleeping arrangements it is. No pressure. Just a chance to get to know each other better, uninterrupted."

"Do you know how seductive a guy with self-control is?"

He laughed. She couldn't possibly know

how his self-control had been careening down the slippery slope toward nonexistence ever since he'd met her.

"I'll let you know," she said.

Axel barked at a squirrel. "Interest in the world again," Jack said. "A good sign."

The three of them walked back to the apartment, the two humans hand in hand.

"NOT SO LOUD!" Selena warned as she and Maxine carried on a conversation in the studio end of the loft. Quinn had left. Drew was in his room, and Selena wasn't eager for him to overhear.

When she'd come home from the walk with Quinn and Axel, she'd found her son sleeping. Peacefully. For the first time in two days. Perhaps sharing your emotional load with someone else was cathartic. She knew she felt better after that surprising cry in the park. Better, perhaps, but not calm. Quinn's unexpected invitation had her in a buzz.

Exhilarated if she'd only admit it.

"You know I'll stay with Drew," Maxine repeated in a whisper.

"After all that's happened, I don't want to

let him out of my sight. Hell, I want to start walking him to school like when he was in kindergarten."

"That's no solution, and you know it."

"But is it right for me to go away?"

"Right to take a little vacation for the first time in your adult life? I'll say it's right. Selena you've been a mother and a provider for twelve years now. You've never been just a little selfish."

"What do you mean? I go places. I have friends. I have a social life."

"Boyfriends, you mean. And everyone of them has merely floated on the surface of your existence. All interchangeable. All disposable. This guy is different."

"That's what scares me. He's become part of my life—I actually called him today instead of you. But, more importantly, he's become a big part of Drew's life. I've never let that happen before. So what if it doesn't work out between Quinn and me? What happens to Drew then?"

"Why do you already have you and Jack broken up before you've even started a relationship? And Drew? Drew's old enough to make and keep friends separate from you."

"So everyone keeps telling me. That's no re-assurance disaster isn't lurking on the horizon."

"Selena Milano! I never took you for a negative person."

"I'm not negative! But I'm trying to be a good parent. To think of all the angles. And here's a little angle lying right below the surface all along, just ready to pop my life raft. Sex."

"What about it?"

"Don't you think Drew's going to wonder—"

"Wonder what, Mom?"

Selena turned to see her son standing a few feet away.

"I'm going to leave you two to talk," Maxine said, heading for the door. "Just remember I'm free this weekend. If you need me."

"What's going on?" Drew asked.

"Let's talk over lunch. Chicken noodle soup okay?"

"I've got chicken noodle soup and orange juice coming out my ears," he replied. "Can we order pizza?"

"You bet." Glad to see his appetite returning, she called for their usual veggie supreme, thin crust.

"What am I supposed to be wondering about?" he asked as she hung up. "And where's Jack?"

Well, there it was. The whole dilemma in a name. And her without a clue as how to present it to her son.

"Is everything okay with Jack?" he persisted.

"Yes. In fact… In fact he's asked me to go away for the weekend. How do you feel about that?"

"How do you want me to feel?"

"I'm not trying to make you feel one way or another. You've been the man in this family for twelve years. You know I've gone on dates. Nothing ever serious. But Quinn… Quinn has the potential to be more than just a date. And I don't want you to think he'd be taking your place in any way."

"Take my place?" Her son grinned. "Mom, be serious. I'm irreplaceable."

"Get over here, and give your mother a hug. No one's looking."

He gave her a big bear hug and a noogie on the top of her head for good measure.

Axel, his tail wagging happily, barked his approval.

"So, kiddo," she said when Drew pulled away self-consciously, "how do you feel about this turn of events?"

"About you and Jack? I admit I didn't want anything to do with him at first. But he grows on you. In fact, with all he knows about dogs and stuff, he's pretty cool. He doesn't try to take over, but he's there for you."

Yeah, she'd found that pretty cool herself.

"And, Mom? I like it best when you're happy. I like Jack, but you should do what makes you happy. Just promise me one thing you won't do this weekend."

"Y-yes?"

"If you're going to have a getaway weekend, don't do wussy stuff like pedicures and mudpacks. Do something awesome like hang gliding or kayaking." With that admonition he began a game of chase with Axel around the apartment.

Selena didn't know if what she felt was a rush of happiness or of trepidation, but she picked up the phone to call Quinn.

CHAPTER THIRTEEN

HE WAS AMAZED at how many times she'd changed her mind before they finally started out for Sonoma and the mountains on Saturday morning. Changed the length of the getaway—they were now down to an overnight. Changed who would pick up whom and where—she'd finally met him at his dog center. Changed which vehicle they were taking and who would be driving. He'd begun to wonder if they'd ever get out of the city.

Now that they were tooling north on Highway 101 under dreary March skies, Jack couldn't help but envision a succession of power struggles on this trip. Yet he held out hope the farther Selena drove her Honda from the city—toward milder temps and a little sun, perhaps—the more she might relax. At least for the weekend. A start.

"Do you want some music?" she asked.

"Background only." He fiddled with the dial until he came up with a cool jazz station, then lowered the volume. "I'd rather talk."

She clutched the steering wheel. "About what?"

"Let's try for ordinary. How's Drew?"

"Better. He did go back to school Thursday, but he keeps asking if anyone's seen Charlie."

"Have they?"

"No. But Sam's acting lookout."

"Is Drew still making deliveries for Sam?"

"Against my better judgment. But Sam, Drew and Maxine ganged up to convince me otherwise."

"I'm with them. Drew needs to carry on."

"So everyone tells me."

He tried to ignore the stiff set of her shoulders, the brusque tone to her answers. "How's Maxine?"

"Maxine has gone totally 'round the bend."

"How so?"

"You remember she said Ted introduced her to a guy at the Midnight Rollers? Some retired businessman? Well, she's seen him every day for a week now. I've never seen her this way before. Giddy. Like a schoolgirl."

"Good for Maxine."

"Easy for you to say. In the past year, I've watched all my close friends pair off and get married, but Maxine? I thought she was a confirmed single. Like me."

"And her new interest bothers you?"

"Well, gee, no. I don't want to sound like I'm trying to rain on anyone's parade. But I feel like I'm out there on Mission Street, twirling my baton, marching south while everyone else is stampeding north."

He ran a finger lightly up her neck to her earlobe. "That's easily rectified."

A loud bang precluded any answer on her part. As the Element shuddered, Selena struggled with keeping the wheel steady, with guiding the vehicle to the shoulder. Forty minutes into what was supposed to be a relaxing getaway, he prepared to change a flat.

"Stay in the car," he said when they finally came to a stop. "I'll take care of it."

"It's my car. I can do it."

"Have you ever changed a tire before?"

"No, but—"

"Now isn't a good first-time opportunity." Wary of traffic, he got out to examine the damage. The right rear tire had blown. Fortunately, the wheel rested on solid ground, away from the cars whizzing by.

She got out right behind him. "At least let me show you where the jack and spare are."

"I thought you hadn't changed a tire before."

"Well, I did read the manual."

"And stayed at a Holiday Inn Express, I presume."

"Very funny." She opened the hatch and lifted out their two duffel bags, then pointed to a compartment door in the floor. "In there. If you insist."

Lifting out the jack and the spare, he nearly tripped over their bags. She hastily moved them into the tall grass next to the shoulder.

"Dammit, Selena! When was the last time you checked your tire tread? All five are nearly bald."

She bristled. "I know they are. New tires are on the must-do list. But the budget—"

"I'm sorry. I didn't mean to snap." He settled in to change the tire. "But I don't like thinking of you with an unsafe ride." He also didn't like thinking of his truck back at the center and idle—with four new tires. "Why did you insist on driving?"

She frowned. "I just thought…you know…heading into uncharted territory, I'd like something familiar around me."

"Come here," he said as gently as possible. "Familiarize yourself with your Honda's lug nuts." He took off his hat and held it out to her. "Hold them in here until I need them again. And don't lose any."

"I have many flaws, sir, but losing things is not among them."

When he'd finally secured the spare tire, he loaded the flat and the jack into the car's back. "We can drop this off at a garage I trust not far from here. How about I finish the drive to Sonoma."

"I'm fine."

"Believe me, I know you are. But I know the way. Once we get off the main road, it's little more than a rough track to the cabin."

"I can handle it."

She'd called him exasperating, but, for sure, he didn't have the market on the trait. "Can you handle taking directions from me?"

"Maybe you have a point." Reluctantly, she moved toward the passenger door.

What was that saying about best laid plans?

He'd intended to pick up boxed picnic lunches at a funky little restaurant he knew just south of Sonoma, then take them to the cabin to eat on the deck with a bottle from his local wine collection and the spectacular view of the meadows and the woods and the mountains.

After dropping off the tire for repair, they did pick up the boxed lunches. But the usual fifteen-minute trip from this point to the cabin turned into an hour-and-a-half nightmare. Seems there was bridge work on the road that led to their turnoff. Two lanes were reduced to one with the weekend crush alternating sides at a crawl. There was no detour. After exclaiming over the first vineyard, Selena became quiet. He understood. It was hard to muster enthusiasm when given a grape-by-grape tour.

And the sun he'd hoped for? Not only did it make its appearance, it bore down on the Element as if trying to poach them inside.

Her stomach growled. "I'm sorry, but I'm starving. Can we eat? It's not as if you're going to have difficulty controlling the car." The speedometer registered ten miles per hour.

"Sure." There went lunch with a view.

They ate in silence, washing down the food with lukewarm bottled water they'd brought from home.

Finally, the familiar private track appeared. As they turned and left the traffic behind to begin the gentle ascent through grasses still winter dry and fragrant, they both breathed more easily. It was midafternoon. The day could be salvaged.

Surprisingly, Selena finally seemed to relax. "This is beautiful!" she exclaimed, rolling down the window and sticking her head out as one of his dogs might do. "And I've always thought of myself as a dyed-in-the-wool city girl."

"Watch out for branches, city girl!" It heartened him to see her come alive again.

It was amazing! Selena had the sensation

of flying. The farther Quinn drove up the track, the farther behind them they put San Francisco, the flat tire and the Sonoma traffic, and the more her spirits soared. She inhaled the pungent fresh air. So this was why people took vacations. And she'd always chalked the phenomenon up to bourgeois conventionality.

As they crossed a creek, Quinn slowed the Element. "There she is."

Tucked in an old stand of oak trees in the middle of a meadow, stood a small, rustic cabin, spring wildflowers spreading outward from its foundation like a lady's skirt, mountains hovering over its roof line like a mantilla.

"The creek runs around the back," he said, "where there's a deck and the requisite California hot tub."

"Clothing optional?"

"Sure. It'll be just you, me and the banana slugs. Not a neighbor for a half-mile radius, and the slugs know how to keep a secret."

"Not a neighbor for a half-mile radius," she mused. "Quite a hunk of prime real estate. Who knew dogs could be so lucrative?"

"It was a gift."

She whistled low. "A gift?"

"A couple—both movie actors—were very grateful I could rehabilitate their extremely unstable German shepherd after the birth of their first child."

"But such a big gift!"

"It was a big dog."

"And big movie stars?"

"Actually, they're just people. Like you and me."

"Minus my outstanding bills, it would seem. So, are you going to tell me who they are?"

"No."

"Dog doctor-patient confidentiality?"

"Something like that."

At that moment Selena found Quinn very, very attractive. A man who didn't need to brag, blab or embellish. My, oh, my.

"Do I get a tour of the cabin?" she asked.

"All three minutes of it." He put the car in gear. "In fact, you can straddle the back door sill and take it all in in less than one."

He was right. The inside of the cabin was one open room—bright and airy, but small—with a sleeping loft. "It's really the land that's the draw," he said. "A lot of times I sleep in a bag on the deck under the stars or pitch a tent in the meadow."

She eyed the loft with its one bed. "Oh, that's why you felt you could offer me separate sleeping quarters."

"There was never any doubt you'd get the bed." He indicated a sofa nestled up to a pot-bellied stove. "My third option."

She was not accustomed to being pursued with restraint.

He led her out onto the back deck with its stunning view of the mountains. "We can hang out here. I have some excellent local wines. Or we can hike. Or…we can go into town."

"Not through that awful traffic again! For better or worse, until we head home, I'm nature girl."

"Then pull up a chair." He nodded toward one of two strange twig creations flanking a *chiminea*. "I'll go get our bags out of the Honda."

She had barely settled into a surprisingly comfortable seat when he came back around the corner of the cabin, scowling.

"There are no bags," he declared.

"Then you must have taken them out when we dropped the flat at the garage."

"No," he said carefully. "I believe you took them out to get to the spare. Back on Highway 101."

"Omigod! I put them in the grass. So you wouldn't trip over them."

"And?"

She jumped from her chair. "I never put them back." She'd clean forgotten. But she did remember how, as she'd held the lug nuts for him, she'd assured him she didn't lose things. He must think her an idiot.

"Well, I hope the clothes you're wearing are comfortable," he said.

"We can't go back for the bags?"

"We might as well head back to San Francisco."

And she was just getting used to the idea of a minivacation.

"Did you have anything of value in your bag?" he asked, pulling her to face him.

"N-no." She didn't want to admit to the condoms she'd slipped in among her clothes. At the last minute. Just in case.

"Sorry I don't have a washer and dryer. Water conservation. Plus, I'm never here long enough." His mouth began to curve in a slow, sensuous grin. "Guess we should put these clothes aside for the trip back. Reduce, reuse, recycle."

"Oh, I bet you're looking forward to the reduction part. Oak leaf, anyone?" She paced the deck. "How could I have been so stupid?"

He caught her as she brushed past him. "Don't beat yourself up," he breathed in her ear. "I keep a few clean T-shirts up in the loft. If you're good, I might loan you one."

Now why did wearing his shirt sound so damned sexy? "You're not angry?"

"Is this a test?" His tone was teasing, but the light in the depths of his eyes was serious. "Did you leave the bags behind deliberately to see what pushes my buttons?"

"We don't know each other very well, do we?"

He led her toward one of the twig chairs, sat, then drew her onto his lap. "I thought that's why we came up here."

"To see if we could get beyond bald tires and lost luggage?"

"For starters." He nuzzled her neck. "And to see if you think camp food's romantic."

"What are you talking about?"

"Just another glitch. I was planning on a little more freedom of movement, but unless you want to brave the construction traffic to have dinner in town, we're going to be eating from the emergency rations I keep here."

"How creative are you with canned goods?"

"I make a mean chuckwagon stew."

She nestled against his chest. Away from San Francisco, away from her friends, she could admit to herself there was something appealing about a man with a backup plan.

"Then there's wine," he added, "but you only get two glasses."

She stuck her tongue out at him. "So when's dinner?"

"Are you hungry already?"

"I'm sorry, but my box lunch didn't fill me up. I'm ravenous. Why do you suppose that is?"

"Some say the wine country air does it. Me, I think it's the thought of my cooking."

"You really can be the loveliest man."

"I thought I was exasperating."

"You are."

"And pushy."

"Yes."

"And—"

"Hut!" She moved in for the kiss.

She came to him.

And, in so doing, made the kiss all the sweeter.

As she pulled away, she ran the tip of her tongue over his mouth. "Do you have a wine for that?"

Frankly, champagne wouldn't do her kisses justice.

"Feed me," she commanded, hopping up and pulling him into the cabin. "You cook. I'll get the wine. Any suggestions?" she asked as she examined the well-stocked rack at the end of the counter in the small galley kitchen.

"It's obvious. Cabernet Sauvignon. It's initials alone cry out for chuckwagon stew." He chose ingredients from the cupboard, began dumping them into a large pot.

"Ah, the manly whir of a can opener," she said as she sidled up to him, wine bottle in hand.

"Save the sarcasm until you've actually

tasted my masterpiece," he ordered, choosing bottled herbs from a small rack. It struck him how pleasurable it was, making a meal for two. "Pour us a couple glasses, but add some to the stew, as well."

"Your secret ingredient?"

"No. That would be the finely chopped banana slug."

"Eeuuw! Why do all males have a fascination with repulsive stuff?"

"It's built into our DNA."

"I believe it. In my close circle of friends, we have seven kids, four of them boys, ranging from five to twelve. That is if you don't count Derrick, who's thirty-four, but still maturing. All of them get the biggest kick out of rude noises, talk of bodily functions and grossing out the girls."

He stopped stirring the pot and looked at her. This was the most specific she'd been about life outside her art and beyond Drew, Maxine and her parents. It was a tiny glimpse into a world of friends she hadn't chosen to introduce to him. He wondered why.

"Do you get together often?" he asked, trying for a neutral tone of voice.

"No." She turned pensive. "We used to see each other more often when we were all single. Margo's Bistro in SOMA became a natural gathering place. But the others met people and married. And now we're lucky if we run into each other over a take-out latte. Imagine four couples married in less than a year. Married." She repeated the word as if she couldn't quite get her tongue around it. "Not a cohabiting twosome among them."

"I know you think divorce statistics are horrible, but studies show married people live longer."

"And do you know how they spend that extra time? Wishing they were single."

He shook his head. "I took you for a realist, not a cynic."

"So you don't believe in taking a relationship for a test drive, so to speak?"

"I think if you're willing to commit to living together, you should be willing to commit. Period."

"Quinn, you are one serious dude."

Quinn. He wondered what it would take for him to hear his given name from her lips.

Their simple supper had already begun to

bubble in the pot. He lifted a spoonful and held it out for her. "Tell me what you think."

She tasted, tentatively, then smiled. "I think you're a master of the canned concoction."

He ladled two bowlfuls. "Inside or on the deck?"

"On the deck. I want to watch the mountains change as the sun sets."

Outside they settled in the twig chairs. "I'm curious," he said. "If you could put an installation on this piece of property, what would it be?"

She sighed deeply, her eyes lighting up. "Absolutely nothing. This site is already fully installed."

At that moment, for her sympathetic insight alone, he knew he'd fallen for her, and hard. Perhaps he should just change his given name to Quinn.

Their backs to the setting sun, they ate and watched the shadows climb the distant mountains, and a rare sense of peace descended upon Selena. "Here," she said, "I don't feel compelled to be the many parts of me. Mother. Artist. Friend. Et cetera. I just *am*."

"There are no ghosts for you here."

She was struck by his choice of words. "Are there ghosts for you?"

"No." He put his empty bowl and spoon on the deck by his chair, then leaned forward, arms on knees, to look her directly in the eye. "I didn't tell you all of why I was given this place. The couple I mentioned met me shortly after Anneka's death. They'd lost a child several years before. They knew my pain and wanted to help in some way."

"They gave you a refuge."

"Yes. I've never let anyone else inside… until you."

What had it cost him to chance this exception?

All this time she'd been worried about what an association with Quinn might cost her. She hadn't given a thought to his ghosts, his vulnerability, his resistance.

And for his courage, she wanted this man. But…

Leaving her chair to sit on his lap, she wound her arms around his neck, kissed his ear, his temple. "The only thing keeping me from your bed is my abject stupidity."

When he looked confused, she explained.

"I…made a purchase before we left the city. For just such a moment as this. But the… package is in my overnight bag."

"Which is in the grass by the side of the road." He didn't look amused. "Perhaps a passing bear can avail himself of your *purchase.* Have himself a little bruin bacchanal."

"I'm sorry." She was. She really, really was.

He stood, dumping her unceremoniously on the decking, then disappeared around the corner of the cabin. Who knew that, after all she'd put him through, the lack of protection would be the very last straw?

Before she could answer her own question, he reappeared, his jacket in hand. Did he want to leave? She could think of nothing she wanted to do less.

He scowled. "You're sorry?" As he unzipped one of the jacket pockets, his scowl turned to a rather seductive grin. "Well, I made a *purchase* before we left the city, too. But, unlike some people, I didn't lose it." With a magician's flourish, he pulled a foil roll of condoms from the depths of the jacket. "What do you think of that?"

She ran across the deck and jumped on him. Legs wrapped around his waist, arms tight about his neck, she whispered in his ear. "I think you're going to be a very busy bear."

The first time, they managed to make it inside, but not as far as the loft. They made love on the sofa. As if they'd invented the act.

The second time started with a dash to the loft stairs and ended with a frenetic tumble in the big bed under the eaves. Who knew laughter could be such an aphrodisiac?

The third time—or did she dream it?—came right before the best night's sleep she'd ever had.

She awoke to the chirping of birds, Quinn's long, muscular body spooned up against her back, his breathing soft against the nape of her neck, his hand resting on her bare hip in a shaft of sunlight. As he slept, she lay very still and studied his hand through her lowered lashes. Strong yet supple, his hands had given her such pleasure last night she finally could envision the Victorian notion of swooning.

He stirred. And wrapped his arm around

her waist, pulling her even closer. "Morning," he breathed in her ear.

Her stomach growled. Okay, it seemed her body kept no secrets from him.

He chuckled.

"What?" she said over her shoulder. "You're not hungry, too?"

"What do you think?"

She could feel hunger of a different sort pressing against her. She could eat in San Francisco, but, once they got back to the real world would she and Quinn ever be able to recapture this closeness, this freedom?

For the fourth time in less than twenty-four hours, she abandoned herself to him.

CHAPTER FOURTEEN

THEY HAD BARELY finished breakfast when Jack began to notice the change in Selena's mood. It started with a call from Drew wanting to know where she'd stored the new bag of dog food. He swore things were fine at home, but when she rang off, she seemed to have stepped through some time-space opening. Her body was still with him in Sonoma, but the rest of her was being pulled back to San Francisco.

"Are you okay?" he asked.

"Yes. It's just that all good things must come to an end."

"That's bullshit." He pulled her to him. "The cabin's here, waiting for us anytime. This… feeling…we get to take back home."

She kissed him with such passion, such urgency, he wondered if she wasn't storing up the feeling. For when she might become unsure. Of him? Of her? Of the strength of what they'd shared?

He wanted to tell her that he was sure enough for the two of them, but the absolute honesty of the night before appeared to be slipping away.

"I'd like to get back to the city," she said. "Maybe stop and see if our duffel bags are still by the side of the road."

She seemed closed to discussion.

When they picked up her repaired tire, he tried to pay, but she absolutely refused to let him. Refused to let him continue driving as well. Heading south on Highway 101, he recognized the spot where they'd had the flat. She made a U-turn. Nothing remained of their overnight bags. As they climbed back into the Element, Jack noted that very little remained of Sonoma Selena. Her standoffish San Francisco persona had begun to reemerge. She called home again.

"Are you sure everything's okay?" he repeated when she hung up, frowning.

"I think so. But Maxine made me promise

to come to the loft before I dropped you off. She wouldn't talk about it over the phone."

"And you think that might mean trouble?"

"With a twelve-year-old and a hundred-pound dog, it could mean anything. I'm lucky to have Maxine."

He might be about to step on a land mine, but he had to know. "Why didn't—don't—your parents help out?"

"I've never asked them to." The stiff set of her shoulders, the tight grip of her fingers on the wheel, told him not to pursue the subject.

Back in the city, when they finally pulled into a parking space not far from her loft, he had the bizarre feeling the overnight at the cabin was nothing more than an illusion.

"I shouldn't be long," she said, getting out of the vehicle.

Oh, no. He wasn't going to be left behind like some minor purchase between errands. He got out right behind her. "Selena, we have to talk."

She glanced up at her apartment windows. "I know what you want me to say. That things are different now. But I'm not sure they are. Sonoma was a beautiful respite.

Like a dream. I don't regret a minute of it." The light in her eyes softened. Saddened. "But this is reality. I have a son. I have responsibilities."

He took her hand. "You don't have to be alone to be a parent. To be responsible. To be strong."

At that moment Drew stuck his head out the window above. "Mom! Jack! Are you guys coming up, or what?"

"I…we're coming," she called back.

Her very small amendment gave Jack hope.

At the top of the stairs they heard movement behind the closed apartment door. A giggle. An answering bark.

"I'm almost afraid to look," she said, unlocking the door and pushing it open.

"Surprise!" The room was packed, wall to wall, with people wearing silly party hats, blowing noisemakers and throwing confetti. Drew and Maxine stood in front of the crowd, grinning gleefully. Jack could see Axel sampling dip from a bowl set on the coffee table.

"What is this about?" Selena exclaimed.

"Your birthday!"

"But that's not until Thursday!"

"Duh!" Drew replied. "You'd be expecting something then. The surprise is the party's now."

"Besides," Maxine added, "it was easier to organize with you out of the loft."

The crowd surged forward, enveloping Selena with hugs, kisses and good wishes. There must have been fifty people in the room, adults and children, but Jack recognized only a few besides Drew and Maxine. Sam from downstairs. The two interns from "Swan Song." And his brother, Ted. As Selena was swept away, four very attractive women surrounded Jack.

One held out her hand. "I'm Nora," she said. "And this is Margo, Rosie and Bailey."

"We're the bistro bunch," Margo said as if he would know all about them. "The children are ours, of course. Our men are…somewhere. Near the food most likely."

"And unless you're the pizza guy," Rosie said, "you must be Jack."

"I am. Jack."

Bailey grinned. "If you don't believe everything Selena's said about us, we won't believe all she's said about you."

Sadly, Selena had said very little about them, and again he wondered why. He caught her eye from across the room. She was the center of an animated group, but she looked worried.

Maxine appeared at his side. "Sorry, girls, he's mine for the moment," she said, pushing him toward Selena's studio end of the apartment. Behind a stack of wooden pallets, she stopped.

"Is this the start of a spy game?" he asked, bemused.

"Sort of. How was Sonoma?"

"Terrific. From my perspective."

"Excellent. Hold on to that thought." She glanced around as if expecting interruption. "I'm going away on a little vacation myself this week. I haven't told Selena yet. Though that's not why I wanted to talk to you."

"You sound serious."

"I am. I know our girl. She has to really care about you to have gone away this weekend. She's never done anything like it before. But now that she's back in the city— her home turf, so to speak—she's going to fight whatever she discovered about herself this weekend. I'm not going to be here, but I want you to promise me you won't let her succumb to her fears."

"Maxine, I wish I could promise you. Selena knows how I feel. She knows what I want. Only she can decide what she wants. I'm not going to force myself on her."

"You're so right for her."

"I think so."

"Then fight for her."

"I'd be fighting Selena herself. Seems counterproductive."

Drew approached with Axel. "Maxine, some guy's at the door, asking for you." The dog had a mustache of dip and chip crumbs. "Cool idea, huh? The party?" Drew asked Jack as Maxine headed for the door. "Did you know it was Mom's birthday?"

"No. That was a surprise to me." As was Selena. Constantly. He searched the room for her, and saw her in conversation with his brother.

"I'm glad Ted could come," Drew said, following Jack's gaze. "He wants to do an article about Mom for his magazine."

Three boys who looked about six years old came barreling toward them. "Drew!" one exclaimed. "Show Casey and Danny Axel's figure-eight."

Drew shrugged. "My public calls."

Jack made his way toward Selena and Ted. Standing behind her, he slipped his arms around her waist, kissed the nape of her neck. "Happy birthday."

She froze in his arms. "It's not till Thursday."

"Oh, that'll give Jack time to think up a great gift," Ted replied, raising Selena's left hand to examine her ring finger. "Something sparkly perhaps?"

"Who's getting something sparkly?" The woman who'd introduced herself as Nora joined the group.

"Would you, please, excuse us?" Selena asked, her tone frosty as she pushed Jack away from the partiers and into Drew's bedroom. She shut the door.

"I'm sorry about all this," she said.

"Why?"

"This can't be fun for you. All these people you don't know."

"I know you. Then there's Drew, Maxine,

Ted and Sam. And I just met Nora, Margo, Rosie and I think it was Bailey. If we went back to the party, I bet I'd meet more."

She lowered her gaze.

"You don't want me to meet more," he said, finally understanding. Finally getting angry. "Some of these people represent your inner circle, and, even after this weekend, you're not ready for me to penetrate that sovereign territory. Your home turf, Maxine calls it."

"It's just that things were going so fast anyway, and the surprise of the party—"

"Excuses, Selena, excuses. We've known each other thirty-four days. Yeah, I'm not ashamed to admit I've kept count. Together we've handled an out-of-control dog, a distraught boy and some personal injury. We shared a weekend. In every sense of the word *share*. Why do you say things are moving too fast when we know, right now, that we're a fit?"

She put her hand over her eyes. "This is so hard."

"Why is it hard?" He pulled her hand away from her face so that she had to look at him.

"Ask your friends who just got married. I bet they say their life is less difficult, not more since they tied the knot."

Although she didn't answer, there was recognition in her wide-eyed look. Then why was she being so damned stubborn?

"Nothing worthwhile is ever really easy," he argued, increasingly frustrated. "Partnering has its moments, but it's a commitment. I'm asking you to take the first step—"

"Toward total vulnerability."

"Knock it off. Vulnerability isn't a four-letter word. Not with someone you can trust. Besides, how can you lay yourself bare with your art, how can you take such big risks in public, but in private you wall yourself off?"

"It's not the same."

"No," he said. "The private stakes are much higher, perhaps. Give a much greater return, too. We made love, Selena. We trusted each other with our whole bodies. How much more vulnerable can you get?"

"Don't pressure me!"

"You can't keep pushing me away, and expect me to always be there. Waiting."

"I know that."

"And you'd still like me to leave?"

"Just give me some space. Some time to catch my breath. If you stay, my friends are going to be in our faces about this weekend. About us."

"And you're not sure there is an *us*."

She looked up at him, her eyes imploring.

What else was there to say? He opened the bedroom door. "I'd better check on the dogs and Andy at the center, anyway. If Ted can't give me a lift, I'll call a cab."

With a sinking heart, he recognized the emotional pink slip he'd been given.

"SELENA?" Maxine poked her head into Drew's bedroom. "I'd like you to meet someone."

Selena brushed the back of her hand over her eyes.

"Are you okay? Where's Jack?" Maxine stepped into the room.

"I'm just tired. And Jack needed to get back to the center. To relieve whoever's on duty."

Maxine gave her a disbelieving look.

"When he made arrangements for the weekend, we weren't expecting this detour at the end. He stayed long enough to be social."

"When I talked to him, he seemed to be settling in for a good time."

"I'm sure he would have, if we'd known about a party in advance." She didn't like getting testy with Maxine, but she didn't want to talk about her real distress. Jack, and how she really felt about him. And whether, in a stupid knee-jerk reaction, she'd pushed him away for good this time.

"Oh, now you're not a fan of surprises?"

"Why tonight of all nights?"

"Because I won't be here Thursday."

"Why not?"

"I'm going away. That's what I've been trying to tell you. That's why I wanted you to meet Lars. Are you still there, sweetie?" she asked poking her head out the door.

A very large, powerful-looking man with a thick shock of faded blond hair stepped into the room. "Selena, I'm so pleased to meet you," he said, extending an enormous paw of a hand. His pale blue eyes twinkled with genuine pleasure.

"I'm afraid I'm at a disadvantage," she said.

"Maxine and I met roller skating," he replied, his voice a deep rumble with a hint of Scandinavia. "But you had already left with an injured wrist. It's better, yes?"

Ah, Maxine's businessman.

"Yes, my wrist is better. And I'm pleased to meet you, too. Are you the reason Maxine won't be here Thursday? Do I remember something about scouting a location for an apiary?"

"Yes. But another time." He put his arm around Maxine, and, although she was dwarfed by his bulk, he seemed to defer to her. "We thought we'd fly to Vegas for some silliness."

"Silliness?"

"You ought to try it sometime," Maxine said, snuggling into the big polar bear of a man. "I thought now would be a good time for me to get away. We're in between projects. You have your community center art classes, but nothing so big the interns couldn't replace me for a while."

"Of course." Had she begun to take her good friend for granted? Selena couldn't remember the last time Maxine had taken time off. "When are you leaving?"

"We thought after your party," Lars replied. "My private jet is fueled and waiting.

Although my Maxine teases me when I say 'my private jet.' For some reason she thinks that it sounds pompous. But it is just good business, even in retirement."

My Maxine?

"Lars doesn't understand I come from another universe," Maxine said with a big grin. "A universe of public transportation."

A protective part of Selena wanted to shake her normally down-to-earth assistant. Wanted to ask if she'd lost her senses. If she really knew what she was doing. A teeny selfish part wanted Maxine right here in San Francisco for the next couple days to help with her own little leap-of-faith crisis.

She looked Lars in the eye. "You take good care of *my* Maxine."

"I have every intention of doing just that."

"Come on, you two," Maxine chided, pulling the both of them out of the bedroom. "You don't need to get into a pissing contest over little old me. There's a birthday party going on, and the birthday girl needs to circulate."

Maxine's comment stunned Selena. Why was she so quick to possess and so loath to be possessed? If she could answer that thorny question, she might be able to solve the dilemma of Jack and her fear of commitment.

MONDAY AFTERNOON found Selena thinking she'd had her fill of being alone. Jack hadn't phoned. Maxine presumably was entrenched in Vegas silliness. Jack hadn't stopped by. Drew had gone to school, then had taken Axel right to Sam's to make deliveries. Jack hadn't acknowledged her existence. Although she had no classes to teach today, she stayed away from SOMA and Margo's Bistro. She didn't want to risk her friends asking why she'd been so distracted during her party last night. And why, after all these weeks, they'd finally gotten to meet Jack only to have him disappear.

Why was that?

After a day spent organizing materials in her studio, she made her way down to her parked Honda, ostensibly to check for a favorite CD, but really to see if Jack had left anything personal behind. He hadn't. But someone had stuck a flyer under her windshield wiper. *Want to catch and keep that man? After only six sessions at Bootsie's Belly Dance Studio, you'll have the sexy skillset necessary!*

Well, wouldn't it be hunky-dory if life were that simple?

As she crumpled up the ad, she saw Drew racing down the sidewalk, arms flailing. "Mom! Is Axel with you?"

"No. Didn't you take him on deliveries?"

"Yes. But Mrs. Bierdermeyer doesn't allow him in her apartment. There's a bench on the sidewalk out front I tie him to. When I came down this time, he was gone. I thought I tied him securely—" His face took on a panicked look.

"Maybe you didn't," Selena said, trying to remain calm. "If he got loose, he'd come home, looking for you or me."

"Or maybe Sam. He's been giving Axel biscuits."

"Then let's see if he's minding the store with Sam."

He wasn't. And Sam hadn't seen him since he and Drew began their deliveries.

"We're going to go look for him," Selena

said. "Will you keep him in the store if he comes back?"

"Of course. I'll make a sign right now and put it next to the register in case any of my customers have seen him. Give me your cell phone number in case he turns up while you're out."

"Good idea." Selena jotted the number on a slip of paper, then dashed after Drew, who was already on the sidewalk calling Axel.

They retraced Drew's delivery route. No dog. It began to rain. Hard. They returned to the Honda to canvas the Mission District by car. Still no dog, and getting more difficult to see by the minute. Although by now Drew was in tears and Selena didn't want to fuel his fears, she suggested they return to the loft to print up some flyers with Axel's picture and contact information. That didn't take much time at all, and they were back on the street, distributing the flyers to local businesses.

Drew had gone from tears to an unnatural stiffness. "Shouldn't we check the animal shelters?"

"I doubt anyone would have turned him in this quickly, but I'll call. We'll definitely go down tomorrow." She regretted those words as soon as she uttered them, as soon as the look of horror suffused her son's features. "He'll come home," she hastened to add, reaching for Drew's hand. He clung. "Even neutered, some dogs like to take off for a spring fling. It'd be just our luck he took off after some cocker spaniel. Lady and the tramp."

"You think?"

"Could be. What I know is Axel has street smarts. He was a Dumpster dog, remember? And he hung in there till Margo rescued him. He'll hang in there this time, too." The only difference this time was the gray hairs she'd have by his return. "We've papered the neighborhood with flyers. Let's go home, get something to eat and see if anyone's left a message on our home phone."

"If he's not back after we've eaten, we'll come back out looking, won't we?"

"Of course."

"Mom...what if—?"

"Don't go there, Drew. Axel's okay." He had to be.

"I meant to say what if we called Jack?"

"Jack can't do any more than we're doing.

Besides, with a whole pack to look after, he's got plenty on his plate. But, honey, we're going to find your dog."

Although Drew didn't look convinced, he didn't argue.

At home there were no messages. Neither she nor he finished the pita sandwiches she made. It was dark when they started out by car again. The rain hadn't let up.

This time Selena drove slowly, and, although she'd never admit as much to Drew, she concentrated on scanning the gutters. For a large, inert form. The thought broke her heart. By eleven o'clock they'd driven up and down every street in the district. Without success. Drew had retreated into miserable silence.

"We're going home now," she said.

"No, Mom! We can't!"

"We're no good if we're dead tired. Besides, Axel's a smart dog. When it started to rain, he probably took cover. Probably dragged a tasty treat from someone's garbage into an empty cardboard box, had dinner and is now snoring away, waiting for the rain to let up before he heads home. And wakes us up in the middle of the night."

"What if he's lost?"

"Dogs have an excellent sense of direction."

"You wouldn't lie to me?"

"Never." Although she'd bend the truth to keep his broken heart at bay.

At home, he wouldn't go to bed until he'd opened several windows. "So we can hear him better," he'd explained. She didn't have the heart to argue, only laid down towels to collect the rain gusting in.

She looked in on him several times during the night. He slept fitfully. She didn't fall asleep until after 5:00 a.m. The doorbell woke her. At eight.

Stumbling out of her bedroom, she saw Drew letting Jack in the apartment.

"I called him, Mom. It's not that I don't think you're doing everything you can. It's just that three's better than two."

CHAPTER FIFTEEN

JACK TRIED TO READ the expression on Selena's face, but couldn't. Perhaps it didn't matter. Although she might not want him part of her inner circle, he wasn't about to let Drew down.

"I have an idea where Axel might be," he said. "But I'll need a recent photo of Drew with Axel if you have one."

"We can use the one we put on the flyers," Drew offered, dashing toward the studio end of the apartment and the computer.

"And I'll get dressed," Selena said. "You can take the photo. I'll take Drew."

"I'm going to need Drew with me if my hunch pans out." When she seemed to be mustering a counterattack, he cut her off. "Drew told me you were going to check the animal shelters this morning."

"You want me out of your way."

"Someone needs to cover the animal shelters."

"Okay." Sighing as though the fight had gone out of her, she headed for her bedroom. He felt no victory. Although she trusted him with her dog and her son, would she ever really trust him? As an integral part of her life.

"Got it!" Drew returned, waving a flyer with a gorgeous photo of Axel and him at play. Jack could feel the love behind the lens. "What now?"

"We look for Charlie." At Drew's puzzled expression, he said, "I'll explain in the truck. Come on. The weather's about to break for the better, and the homeless will be on the move."

Down below on the street, he checked on the four dogs in the large custom pen in the back of the truck.

"Why'd you bring them?" Drew asked.

"You'll see." Hopefully.

Under way, he handed Drew a city map on which he'd circled a half-dozen locations surrounding the Mission District. "As we check each spot," he said, "you cross it off."

"Why are we looking for Charlie?"

"Because Axel is enough like Pip in size alone that Charlie may have taken him." Either on purpose or out of delusion.

"How do you know about these places?" Drew asked, indicating the circles Jack had drawn on the map.

"One of the things we do from my center is cruise the city in an attempt to monitor the dog population with the homeless. Checking on the welfare of the dogs is an unobtrusive way of monitoring the homeless, too. There are certain spots they congregate in bad weather."

"Do you know Charlie?"

"Not personally. I'll need you to point him out."

"I never did anything mean to him. Why do you think he took Axel?"

"If he did take your dog, it probably wasn't personal. Charlie would have seen Axel sitting on the sidewalk, there for the taking. Like a half-eaten burger in the garbage. It would have been pure opportunity."

"Right up until the accident," Drew replied,

hope in his words, "Charlie took good care of Pip."

"If Axel's with him, he'll be okay." Jack didn't like making promises he couldn't keep, but he saw no point in trotting out a worst-case scenario. Not with a sensitive twelve-year-old. A twelve-year-old who was beginning to feel like a son.

Without luck, they checked three of the locations he'd pinpointed. As the weather improved and the homeless dispersed, it became less and less likely they'd catch up with Charlie unless he returned to Drew's neighborhood. But if Charlie knew he'd taken someone else's dog, he'd avoid that area. There were too many unknowns to make an assessment or offer further encouragement. Silence was the only comfort he could offer, and this kid with an aching heart, on vigilant look-out in the passenger seat, seemed all right with that.

"There he is!" Drew suddenly exclaimed. "And he has Axel with him! Let me out!"

"Calm down," Jack replied, reaching over to lay a restraining hand on the boy. "We have to be careful how we handle this." He pulled his truck over and parked. "You understand how important this is. Will you trust me to do the talking at first? Will you follow my lead?"

"If it'll get Axel back, yeah."

"Bring the photo."

They got out of the truck and walked toward Charlie. Avoiding eye contact, the man continued his forward shuffle, pushing a beat-up shopping cart to which Axel was connected by his leash. The dog spotted Drew and began to dance about, barking joyously.

With a shake of his head, Jack indicated Drew shouldn't rush to reclaim his pet. "Charlie?" he said, stopping at a respectful distance.

Charlie halted, but didn't look up. Axel's tail looked as if it was about to wag off, and Drew's whole body hummed with longing. Jack could feel the emotion sizzle from the boy's shoulder right into his own hand. But, as promised, Drew didn't move, didn't say a word.

"We're glad you've found our dog," Jack began. As if catching on to his intentions, Drew held up the flyer with the clear photo of Axel and himself. "As you can imagine, the boy was some worried. But we're here now to offer you the reward."

Charlie's head popped up for a second, before he looked toward his shoes. "This is my Pip," he mumbled.

"I know you lost your dog," Jack continued, keeping his voice even, "and we understand your pain. But if you help us, we can perhaps help you."

"Don't need your money."

"Okay. But how about we help you find a new dog of your own."

"Got a dog. Pip here."

"Charlie," Drew said softly, his voice catching, "please, look at the picture. You found Axel. My dog."

Something in Drew's plea seemed to touch the man. He cocked his head to look sideways at the offered flyer.

"Will you do one thing for us?" Jack asked. "Then we'll leave you alone."

"Wha's that?"

"Let the dog off his leash. He'll tell us who his owner is."

Charlie seemed to think long and hard about this proposition. Then, as if in slow motion, he unhooked Axel's leash from his collar. No sooner had he done so than the dog catapulted toward Drew, knocking him to the pavement and covering him with dog kisses.

The life seemed to go out of Charlie, deflating his already sorry demeanor.

Jack couldn't waste the momentum. Leaving Drew to Axel's ministrations, he concentrated on the woebegone man before him. "Charlie, that's my truck over there. I'd like you to meet four dogs from my center. I know I can't replace Pip, but maybe one of those dogs would make you a decent companion."

"You'd give me a dog?"

"And some food. For both of you. And my card. If you ever felt you needed help caring for the dog." He made the offer, knowing there were people who'd think he was a fool. Or irresponsible. Or worse. He wasn't. He was a realist. He couldn't eradicate homelessness, but he could, in some instances, provide a small comfort the soup kitchens and shelters couldn't. He could foster the intangible bond humans formed with animals. A bond that saved some from the dark abyss.

He led Charlie to the back of his truck where four of his dog pack waited, tongues lolling happily.

Surprisingly, the three bigger dogs were not the ones Charlie gravitated toward. Instead, his face softened at the sight of the one-eyed Chihuahua that had refused to be left behind at the center. The tiny dog that had scrambled up boxes to get into the pickup bed and had refused to get out. Until now. When Jack opened the pen door, she fairly flew into Charlie's arms. A grin split Charlie's weathered and bruised face as he tucked the slip of a dog into his overcoat. Jack loaded a small carton of dog food, water and camp-style rations into Charlie's shopping cart, along with a half-dozen business cards, then motioned to Drew and Axel, who were playing an exuberant game of fetch with a stick.

Wordlessly, Charlie moved on, but Jack felt hopeful he now wouldn't shy away from the center truck when Jack or one of his staff made their rounds.

Axel piled into the cab with the two of them. Normally, Jack made it a rule the dogs rode in back. This time he made a happy exception. Within minutes on the ride home, Axel, looking none the worse for wear, fell asleep at Drew's feet.

"Jack? Thank you."

"No thanks necessary, Drew." If any were, they should go the other way. At one point in his life, Jack had sunk to a level not far from Charlie's. At least emotionally. A level of stark disengagement. His dogs had kept him from the abyss. But it had taken one particular dog, a woman and this guileless boy to make him feel connected again. To life. And to its many possibilities.

EAGERLY, Selena waited on the sidewalk in front of her apartment. In the middle of the sad task of checking the animal shelters, she'd received the call from Drew telling her they'd found Axel. How had Quinn known where to look when she hadn't?

"Mom! We're back!" With matching grins on their faces, her son and his dog came barreling down the sidewalk toward her. Quinn loped along behind, making no attempt this time to have either boy or animal conform to dog-walking etiquette.

A few feet from her, Axel reared up on his hind legs and planted his front paws on her shoulder. For once, she didn't resist his sloppy kisses. "We sure missed you!"

"Jack knew right where he'd be!" Drew exclaimed. "And Charlie now has a new friend. A Chihuahua, can you believe it?"

She could believe almost anything if it pertained in the slightest to Jack Quinn. He was full of surprises. "You need to go see Sam," she said instead. "He's been worried about you two."

"Come on, boy!" Drew's face showed the unabashed joy that warmed a parent's heart.

When they were alone, she turned to Quinn. "Thank you," she said.

"I don't want your thanks."

"Then how about lunch?"

"I don't want lunch, either."

She thought about how she'd treated him Sunday evening at her surprise birthday party. She'd been wrong about that. Furthermore, by distancing him, she'd put herself in a place she really didn't want to be. "Look, Quinn…can we take this a day at a time?"

"What *this?*"

He wasn't making matters any easier. "Us."

"You admit there is an *us?*"

"Y-yes. But I'd like us to explore that concept slowly."

"Sorry. Don't want that. Don't have the time."

Okay, now he was making her mad. "What do you want, then?"

He reached out and grasped her upper arms, turned her so she had to look squarely at him. "I don't want happiness meted out in stingy portions. I want to grab the whole enchilada. Swallow it whole. The moment and the promise of the future. I want to do what feels absolutely right. And if you won't admit what that is, you're a much more stubborn woman than I thought."

He released her, then walked away. Again. Who did this guy think he was? Some guru, handing out cosmic riddles? Well, she was not Little Grasshopper. She would not say, "How high?" when he said, "Jump."

"Mom?" Drew and Axel came up beside her. "Where's Jack?"

"Gone."

"Why?"

"It wasn't going to work out," she said, making her way up the stairs to the loft, her legs feeling leaden, her mind stuffed with cotton batting.

"What wasn't going to work out?" Drew asked, a panicky hitch in his voice.

In the apartment, she turned to him. "A relationship. Between Quinn and me."

"So you're just going to ditch him the way you ditched my father?" he screamed.

"Don't speak to me that way."

"What way? Truthfully? What's wrong with you having a relationship with Jack?"

"He doesn't want just a relationship. He wants marriage. A family life."

"Oh, and that's the worst thing that could possibly happen to you! To us!" he shouted. Axel began to whine. "Sometimes you are so dumb."

"What's so dumb about our life now? Just the two of us? I'm sick and tired of everybody around me making single-parenthood seem like a stupid disease."

"I'm a kid, but even I know that's not what they're doing."

"So enlighten me, smart guy."

"They're talking about knowing a good deal when it's standing right in front of you. Jack's a good deal."

In the face of this twelve-year-old's certainty, she felt buried in obstinacy, but couldn't find an escape route.

"Mom, why won't you let him love you?"

Were they talking about love? Stunned, she stared at her man-child. "What makes you think Quinn loves me?"

"I'm not blind." He swiped at his eyes. "And I can see you love him, too. But you won't admit it."

When she couldn't find words to answer, he added, "If I had Jack as a dad, I wouldn't have to look any further, would I? For my biological father."

"That's called emotional blackmail, mister."

"No, it's not. It's reality. Something you're always telling me to accept. Know what else you're always telling me? Not to cut off my nose to spite my face. Maybe you should follow your own advice."

He took off for his room, Axel following. Selena waited for the door to slam, but it didn't. This was no tantrum. Was the matter of

Jack Quinn so important to Drew, then, that he was truly trying to issue her a wake-up call?

She stomped into the kitchen. Her son might be showing surprising signs of maturity, but that didn't mean she had to. Childishly, she banged pots and pans just for the noise. Unfortunately, the noise didn't drown out the tiny, annoying voice in her head that said maybe her son was right.

She was a risk-taker, dammit. So why did she fear this commitment Quinn wanted? She thought back on the difficulties her coffee house friends had encountered on the road to love. All of them—Margo, Nora, Derrick, Bailey and Rosie—had taken the leap of faith despite early fears. Fear of failure. Fear of looking the fool. Fear of losing oneself. Those were all fears Selena faced—and conquered—every day as a single-parent living in a city more hospitable to raising dogs than children, and as an artist swimming out of the mainstream.

What had Jack said to her once? You can still be strong and be part of a couple? Dared she believe him? Hadn't she already shown a belief in him by allowing him to work his magic with Axel? And with Drew? Had she become weaker in the process? No. If anything, her life had become richer, more prone to detours and discoveries.

Besides, she had to admit stubborn self-reliance didn't keep her especially warm on damp San Francisco nights. In Sonoma, Quinn had.

And right now she couldn't picture him not in her future.

What was she going to do now? It was so obvious.

"Drew!" She raced to the studio end of the loft and began a frantic search for a tarp, a four-inch brush and red paint. It had to be red. An epiphany deserved red. "Come help me before it's too late!"

He appeared outside his bedroom. "Only if it's going to bring Jack back."

"If it doesn't," she replied with a thudding heart, "I totally misread his message." Supplies in hand, she hurried from the apartment.

"Can Axel come?"

"For better or worse, he's part of the package."

Drew grinned. All the way to Quinn's

canine center. But when she got out of the Honda and headed to the building directly across the street, he resisted. "Aren't you going to talk to Jack?"

"First things first."

And the first thing was convincing one of the apartment dwellers opposite Quinn's place to buzz her up and give her access to the building's roof. Drew looked as if he might actually explode from excitement as he listened to her plea and caught on to her intent.

"Okay," the disembodied man's voice said, "I'll buzz you up. But if you're not legit, may they put on my tombstone, 'He died a sucker for romance.'"

Buzzed through, Selena headed for the roof, followed by Drew and Axel. On the landing, a man—most likely the one who'd let them in—peered through a cracked door, the safety chain firmly in place. "It's all right," Drew assured him, "my mom's an installation artist, and this is going to be her best piece yet."

On the roof, Drew tied Axel to an exposed pipe, then opened the paint can and helped her spread the tarp. But he let her paint the message. He seemed to know this was something she had to commit to on her own. When she'd painted the final letter, she had him help her hang the tarp over the edge of the building, facing the dog center.

"No turning back now," she said. "Take Axel across the street. Get Quinn to come outside."

"You bet!" Drew gave her a bone-crushing hug and a big smacking kiss on the cheek before he untied Axel and ran downstairs.

She paced the roof and wondered if she'd lost her mind completely or finally found it.

JACK—trailed by his entire staff—followed Drew out onto the sidewalk. He had no idea what had gotten into the kid—he wouldn't even explain how he happened to be in the neighborhood without his mother—but he sure seemed excited.

"Look!" Drew commanded, pointing across the street.

Before anything else, Jack saw her. Selena. On the opposite building's roof, of all places. Leaning over the half wall, she indicated a large banner that hadn't been there when he'd come back to the center. She hadn't mentioned doing an installation in his neighborhood.

"Read it!" she shouted.

He did. In enormous caps, the banner read JACK, WILL YOU MARRY ME? SELENA.

"Are you serious?" It wasn't the most romantic response, but it was the most honest.

"Read it again!"

He started to, then stopped. She'd called him Jack. She had to be serious.

"So I'm absolutely sure you mean it," he shouted, "you have to come to me!" For a moment he thought he might have pushed her too far.

Only for a moment.

She disappeared from the roof, emerging long minutes later on the sidewalk below. Merely glancing both ways, she dashed across the street. And into his arms.

"Well?" she asked, breathless.

"This isn't just a quirky installation?"

"No!"

"Good. I wouldn't be satisfied being a temporary part of the landscape."

Her arms linked behind his neck, she

leaned back and bestowed upon him an almost blinding smile. "I was thinking of moving beyond temporary works. In fact, I was thinking of investing in something more like, say…old masters."

"Are you calling me old?"

"Just old enough to know what's good for you. Maybe for the both of us."

"Us. I like that word."

"I admit, it has potential to become my new favorite."

"Guys!" Drew pleaded. "Can we get back to the question?"

"Hear, hear!" the center staff chorused.

Both Jack and Selena laughed. "The impatience of youth," he said.

"I must be young at heart," she remarked, anticipation lighting her features. "I'd like to know your answer, too."

"Yes. That's my answer. Was there ever any doubt?"

The peanut gallery cheered.

He kissed her long and hard. "I love you, Selena."

"I love you, too, Quinn."

"All I get is one *Jack?*"

She cocked her head. "First names are so intimate. From now on, I think I'm going to have to save yours for strictly private celebrations."

He looked forward to countless occasions to come.

EPILOGUE

HOLDING A BOX of sparklers, Selena stood apart from the rowdy group of friends and family cavorting on Ocean Beach, and watched the sun begin its descent toward the Pacific horizon. What an absolutely glorious picnic day this had been. And the most startling part was yet to come.

She and Jack were getting married.

In just a few minutes. Yet only the two of them knew this would be the time and place. Well, the two of them and the justice of the peace Jack was right now fetching from the parking lot. Sure, she knew that an impromptu marriage on a beach at sunset was a cliché. But both she and Jack agreed it felt right. Where else could dogs be guests?

Marriage. A word in a foreign language she was learning to embrace. In the past few

months she'd learned to embrace many surprising new concepts. And let go several
outworn ideas she'd once held fast.

A Frisbee whizzed by her head, chased by
a half-dozen dogs from Jack's center and the
preteens from the Margo's Bistro pack. Drew,
Leslie and Ellie. There was real kid joy in their
play, but a hint of adolescent flirtation as well.

The adults, spread out over the sand, were
engaged in their own amusements. Rosie and
Hudson—Hud, the newly elected mayor of
San Francisco, no less—were engaged in a
spirited political discussion with her college
interns, Ted, and Ted and Jack's mother,
who'd come from Arizona at Jack's request.
Nora's Erik was involved in a wickedly com-
petitive game of volleyball with the canine
center staff. Nora, four months pregnant and
glowing, stood on the sidelines and cheered
with abandon. Margo and Robert supervised
a grill as the younger children—Peter,
Danny, Savannah and Casey—toasted
marshmallows. And Maxine and Lars stood
at the water's edge, nuzzling as if they were
the only two people in the western hemi-
sphere. The setting sun glinted off the

matching wedding bands on their entwined hands. Apparently, what happened in Vegas didn't always stay in Vegas.

"Darling, your friends are marvelous!"

"She always did surround herself with good people. Always had an innate sense of how to build a world for herself. Our strong girl."

Selena turned at the sound of Berta's and Rocco's voices. Her parents had flown halfway around the globe to be here. Because she'd asked them. How simple was that?

Actually, not simple at all.

Jack had almost refused to marry her when she'd said she wasn't going to call her parents home. He'd said he thought they deserved to meet her future husband and he, them. She'd said they hadn't come back before, and he'd countered with, "Have you ever asked them?" She hadn't.

But when she finally did, she was shocked at how eagerly they accepted, making her wonder if maybe she'd been a little off-putting herself in her resolved self-reliance. All her life she boasted she had what she needed. Jack was teaching her she had a right to act on her wants, as well.

That Jack.

"You know what I was thinking?" Berta linked arms with Selena. "I think this is the perfect moment for a wedding."

"Couldn't keep a secret, huh?" With a grin splitting his handsome features, Jack strode up, justice of the peace in tow.

"I didn't tell. They just knew." Selena stood on tiptoe to plant a kiss on Jack's chin. Maybe people who loved each other, who made a commitment to each other, had a sixth sense about others prepared to take that same path. Or maybe, happy, they simply wished a comparable happiness on others.

"Shall we act surprised?" Rocco asked.

"Are you?"

"No, sweetie. We raised you to know yourself and be open to possibilities. We're not surprised, but we couldn't be more pleased." He gave his daughter a huge hug.

"Come on, Rocco," Berta urged, taking the sparklers from Selena's hands. "The least we can do is round up the others. I don't think any one of this family of friends would want to miss this event."

So, as their two-footed and four-footed

dearly beloved gathered around them and the sun dipped into the Pacific, Selena Milano cast off her stubbornly-single status and took Jack Quinn to be her husband as he took her to be his wife. In the end it was so traditional as to be awesomely cutting edge.

She couldn't wait for the next installation.

* * * * *

THE ROYAL HOUSE OF NIROLI
Always passionate, always proud

The richest royal family in the world—united by blood
and passion, torn apart by deceit and desire

Nestled in the azure blue of the Mediterranean Sea, the
majestic island of Niroli has prospered for centuries. The
Fierezza men have worn the crown with passion and
pride since ancient times. But now, as the king's health
declines, and his two sons have been tragically killed, the
crown is in jeopardy.

The clock is ticking—a new heir must be found before
the king is forced to abdicate. By royal decree the inter-
nationally scattered members of the Fierezza family are
summoned to claim their destiny. But any person who
takes the throne must do so according to The Rules of
the Royal House of Niroli. Soon secrets and rivalries
emerge as the descendents of this ancient royal line vie
for position and power. Only a true Fierezza can become
ruler—a person dedicated to their country, their people…
and their eternal love!

Each month starting in July 2007,
Harlequin Presents is delighted to bring you
an exciting installment from
THE ROYAL HOUSE OF NIROLI,
in which you can follow the epic search
for the true Nirolian king.
Eight heirs, eight romances, eight fantastic stories!

Here's your chance to enjoy a sneak preview of
the first book delivered to you by royal decree…

FIVE minutes later she was standing immobile in front of the study's window, her original purpose of coming in forgotten, as she stared in shocked horror at the envelope she was holding. Waves of heat followed by icy chill surged through her body. She could hardly see the address now through her blurred vision, but the crest on its left-hand front corner stood out, its *royal* crest, followed by the address: *HRH Prince Marco of Niroli...*

She didn't hear Marco's key in the apartment door, she didn't even hear him calling out her name. Her shock was so great that nothing could penetrate it. It encased her in a kind of bubble, which only concentrated the torment of what she was suffering and branded it on her brain so that it could never be forgotten. It was only finally pierced by the sudden opening of the study door as Marco walked in.

"Welcome home, *Your Highness*. I suppose I ought to curtsy." She waited, praying that he would laugh and tell her that she had got it all wrong, that the envelope she was holding, addressing him as Prince Marco of Niroli, was some silly mistake. But like a tiny candle flame shivering vulnerably in the dark, her hope trembled fearfully. And then the look in Marco's eyes extinguished it as cruelly as a hand placed callously over a dying person's face to stem their last breath.

"Give that to me," he demanded, taking the envelope from her.

"It's too late, Marco," Emily told him brokenly. "I know the truth now…." She dug her teeth in her lower lip to try to force back her own pain.

"You had no right to go through my desk," Marco shot back at her furiously, full of loathing at being caught off-guard and forced into a position in which he was in the wrong, making him determined to find something he could accuse Emily of. "I trusted you...."

Emily could hardly believe what she was hearing. "No, you didn't trust me, Marco, and you didn't trust me because you knew that I couldn't trust you. And you knew that because you're a liar, and liars don't trust people because they know that they themselves cannot be trusted." She not only felt sick, she also felt as though she could hardly breathe. "You are Prince Marco of Niroli.... How could you not tell me who you are and still live with me as intimately as we have lived together?" she demanded brokenly.

"Stop being so ridiculously dramatic," Marco demanded fiercely. "You are making too much of the situation."

"Too much?" Emily almost screamed the words at him. "When were you going to tell me, Marco? Perhaps you just planned to walk away without telling me anything? After all, what do my feelings matter to you?"

"Of course they matter." Marco stopped her sharply. "And it was in part to protect them, and you, that I decided not to inform you when my grandfather first announced that he intended to step down from the throne and hand it on to me."

"To protect me?" Emily nearly choked on her fury. "Hand on the throne? No wonder you told me when you first took me to bed that all you wanted was sex. You *knew* that was the only kind of relationship there could ever be between us! You *knew* that one day you would be Niroli's king. No doubt you are expected to marry a princess. Is she picked out for you already, your *royal* bride?"

* * * * *

Look for
THE FUTURE KING'S PREGNANT MISTRESS
by Penny Jordan in July 2007,
from Harlequin Presents,
available wherever books are sold.

HARLEQUIN®
Live the emotion™

American ROMANCE

Heart, Home & Happiness

HARLEQUIN®

Blaze™

Red-hot reads.

HARLEQUIN®

EVERLASTING LOVE™

Every great love has a story to tell™

Harlequin® Historical
Historical Romantic Adventure!

HARLEQUIN®

HARLEQUIN ROMANCE®

From the Heart, For the Heart

HARLEQUIN®

INTRIGUE

Breathtaking Romantic Suspense

Medical Romance™...
love is just a heartbeat away

**There's the life you planned.
And there's what comes next.**

HARLEQUIN®
Presents
Seduction and Passion Guaranteed!

HARLEQUIN®
Super Romance®

Exciting, Emotional, Unexpected

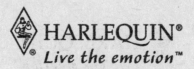

HARLEQUIN®
INTRIGUE®

BREATHTAKING ROMANTIC SUSPENSE

Shared dangers and passions lead to electrifying romance and heart-stopping suspense!

Every month, you'll meet six new heroes who are guaranteed to make your spine tingle and your pulse pound. With them you'll enter into the exciting world of Harlequin Intrigue— where your life is on the line and so is your heart!

THAT'S INTRIGUE—
ROMANTIC SUSPENSE
AT ITS BEST!

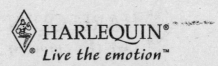

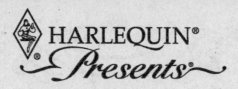

HARLEQUIN®
Presents®

The world's bestselling romance series...
The series that brings you your favorite authors,
month after month:

Helen Bianchin...Emma Darcy
Lynne Graham...Penny Jordan
Miranda Lee...Sandra Marton
Anne Mather...Carole Mortimer
Susan Napier...Michelle Reid

and many more uniquely talented authors!

Wealthy, powerful, gorgeous men...
Women who have feelings just like your own...
The stories you love, set in exotic, glamorous locations...

HARLEQUIN®
Presents®

Seduction and Passion Guaranteed!

www.eHarlequin.com

HPDIR104

Harlequin® Historical
Historical Romantic Adventure!

Imagine a time of chivalrous knights and unconventional ladies, roguish rakes and impetuous heiresses, rugged cowboys and spirited frontierswomen—— these rich and vivid tales will capture your imagination!

Harlequin Historical... they're too good to miss!

SPECIAL EDITION™

Emotional, compelling stories that capture the intensity of living, loving and creating a family in today's world.

Desire

Modern, passionate reads that are powerful and provocative.

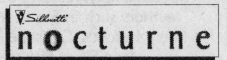

Dramatic and sensual tales of paranormal romance.

Romances that are sparked by danger and fueled by passion.

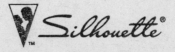